HER LAWFUL MASTER

Pleasure Island Book Four

ANYA SUMMERS

Published by Blushing Books
An Imprint of
ABCD Graphics and Design, Inc.
A Virginia Corporation
977 Seminole Trail #233
Charlottesville, VA 22901

Anya Summers
Her Lawful Master

EBook ISBN: 978-1-947132-01-6
Print ISBN: 978-1-682591-38-3

Cover Art by ABCD Graphics & Design
This book contains fantasy themes appropriate for mature readers only.
Nothing in this book should be interpreted as Blushing Books' or the author's
advocating any non-consensual sexual activity.

Chapter 1

October

I f she had to title the scene like one of her pieces, she'd call it 'A Master & His Domain,' what with Jared peering over his creation looking like the epitome of Alpha Dom in his tailored gray pinstripe slacks and mint green dress shirt, the sleeves artfully rolled up on his muscular forearms.

"It's quite the view," she said, taking a few snapshots. Her digital camera clicked through the frames at a rapid pace. Perhaps there'd be a winner in the bunch. But, more likely, it would give her a starting point to springboard from—a set of images she could study to discern what the best potential angles might be.

"Yeah, I think so too," Jared murmured with a proud expression on his strong face, his ginger hair framing him, And, well, why not? The Dom had done a remarkable job with the island getaway. He should be pleased. It was the realization of a dream, and a kinky hideaway for those in the BDSM lifestyle that Piper had yet to explore.

She liked Jared. He was a damn fine Dom. He was a few

years younger than she, considering the fact that she was staring down the double barrel of forty in a few months, but his confidence tended to overshadow his younger age. If only Piper were a few years younger. She sighed to herself.

There were a lot of what-ifs and if-onlys when it came to her single status. What if she had or hadn't done things this way or that? It was enough to drive her to drink. At least she'd avoided the curse of the crazy cat lady syndrome. So that was something, although it was a road she could still traverse here if she weren't careful. Mentally shaking herself, Piper considered the myriad ways in which she could approach this job and asked, "I know we had tossed a few ideas back and forth via email, but did you end up having a direction in mind for the brochure?"

"Why don't we have a seat? I do have an image in my mind of what I would like, but I'm not sure I can translate it so you will understand, lass," Jared said, and gave her one of his blazing smiles. Happiness seemed to permeate his being as he reclined behind his grand wooden desk, looking every inch a powerful Master, and there was a calmness to his energy that hadn't been there previously. In fact, the last time she'd run into him at Declan and Zoey's wedding, he'd appeared depressed to her—at least, that was what had come through her camera lens. His normal exuberant flair for life seemed to have been diminished. Piper suspected it was his new sub Naomi putting the blissful expression on his face.

"Well, how much input do you want from me?" she asked, sitting on the soft leather chair opposite him. It was one of those chairs that you sank into and never wanted to leave. While she could get comfortable anywhere, and had on occasion slept in the bush as comfortably as she had in a five-star resort, she did enjoy the creature comforts more and more. Probably an age thing she didn't want to contemplate too much. Jared and Pleasure Island were her customers, which meant that, at the end of the day, what he preferred was what she would deliver, even if it went against her aesthetic and artistic sense or she creatively preferred a different angle. He was paying, therefore, this was his project. Although she wouldn't issue a horrible product, no matter if stylistically it wasn't her cup of tea.

"As much as you will give me. I know how gifted you are, and if you say to head in one direction versus another, then I will trust your guidance. I want the brochure to make the expansion of the place into new markets, to entice the individuals in those venues to visit. In order for the island to truly be sustainable and turn a profit, I need customers to come. The opening fanfare has been stellar, however, before I will declare it a success, we need both repeat and new business. I want the brochure to convey why this is the only destination spot for those in the lifestyle to experience a bit of exotic R&R with all the convenience of it being lifestyle friendly," Jared said, leaning back in his chair.

Sublime pleasure suffused her veins at his compliment. It never failed to amaze her that she was able to work in a profession she loved and get paid rather handsomely for it. Having her talent recognized by Jared was the cherry and whipped cream on top of an already blessed life. Being given freedom to express her creativity and proceed with her gut instincts for a shoot made Piper salivate over the upcoming project. It was like letting a child loose in a candy store and saying, 'have at it, kid.'

"I appreciate your confidence in my work." She studied his office. It was comprised of sleek lines and elegance, very much like the man himself, with nothing out of place, but it was also a room full of comfort, from the buttery soft leather chairs to his expansive desk and his chair, a full service coffee and tea station, to pastries from the chef made for Jared. These were added touches she'd noticed in the lobby as well. This resort, from what she'd viewed of the hotel and his office so far, was chock full of understated elegance and extra touches that went above and beyond the normal fare found elsewhere. In her mind, the brochure for Pleasure Island needed to be an extension of those items.

When it came to people in the lifestyle, they didn't need to see more tits and ass. They saw that at any club. Their community was rife with people who didn't restrain themselves from living out their fantasies, and that was what was needed to entice them. The fantasy of the island was the key to marketing it: making people desperate to visit and, more importantly, demonstrating what fantasy the island could allow them to experience that their local club or home could not.

"You know, Jared, why don't I approach this from two angles, and make more than one mock up? Then you can decide which choice is best for you. From what you explained in your email, you want something that is going to entice the higher end lifestylers to the island, but then also have sale weeks for those who can't afford the regular full price."

"That's correct. And I did send you a list of clubs that we've opened the doors to in order to expand our base of operations. Working in cooperation with the owners in those clubs, we have already vetted the majority of their members. Now it's about getting them to come here."

"Well, I think I can help you with that. In my opinion, I think the best way to proceed, especially knowing the owners at *Allure*, *Underworld*, and *Cuffs and Spurs*, along with their memberships, is to play up the elegance of Pleasure Island. Show them why it's a must-see destination for those in the lifestyle and what they might experience here that they cannot at home, in a tasteful package."

Jared contemplated her with his intense jade eyes, his hands steepled under his chin as his mind worked out the angles. Then he said, "I like it, Piper. Let's try it your way first. If need be, we can reassess in a few days."

"Absolutely. If there's another direction that you feel is better for you and the island, I'm open to your input and direction, as much as you want to give me. I can get started photographing right away and will have the first few mock-ups in a handful of days."

"That's good. I like your efficiency on this. Just so that you are aware, you will have full access to every part of the island: the villas, pool, marina, restaurant, club. You name it, you can photograph it. Anything but the guests—and that, lass, is non-negotiable. We value our guests' privacy and safety above all else, so I cannot have you film them, but the rest of the island is your oyster, so to speak."

Those words were literally music to her ears. Piper wanted to tap dance around his office at her little victory. It was like she'd been handed keys to the kingdom with the all-access pass to shoot as she wanted, where she wanted, and when. From what she'd viewed of the island so far, she might even get a few pieces to add to her gallery in Santa Barbara. Piper was as pleased as punch that this job was turning into a win-win scenario with potentially huge payoffs. "And that's something that I will be sure to include in the mock ups: the privacy and safety portion. I have your key points that you want listed on the brochure. If you have literature you want included, email that to me. I may need to edit a bit for space but you will have final approval on every aspect of the finished product. Don't worry about the images, I will take more than enough pictures so when we are deciding what should be included in the brochure, you will not want for selection but will have an overabundance to choose from."

"That's perfect, lass. And my secretary is adding the amend-ment to the contract like you requested. As long as I sign off on the prints you decide to use for your gallery, I love the idea. Might even have to purchase one or two of the images myself."

The man certainly was a charmer. Was it any wonder his staff adored him? She said, "They would be a gift for you, Master J, I wouldn't charge you to make a print or two with your more than generous fee for doing this job. With the amendment added to our agreement, you would receive a royalty of twenty percent for any image I develop and display for sale at my gallery, Phoenix Rising in Santa Barbara, but for the others, pish-posh."

He chuckled, a deep-throated bark and said, "Thank you, I appreciate it. Maybe I could interest you in taking a photograph of my sub and me."

"I'd be delighted to do a portrait shoot. Just let me know when you would like it done and we can put it into my agenda while I'm here," Piper said.

"Great, we'll make arrangements for that. I had my staff put you in one of the private villas, number five, so you can have privacy to create. One of the bellhops—Sean, I believe—has already delivered your suitcases. You will have a cart at your disposal while you're here, to take you and your camera equipment anywhere you want to go on the island. If you give me five minutes, we can get started on our tour. I have one more individual joining us. I hope that's all right. He just needs to do a bit of an inventory of the property for legal purposes."

"No. I don't mind at all," she said, to prove she was as publicly relatable as possible, even though she did mind the intrusion. She would have far preferred the chance to scope out the island without interference, but she'd deal with the complication and do her own tour later without anyone present. This was all formalities for the job. Jared was paying her a pretty penny to put together this brochure, so if he wanted her to do headstands while she took photos, she'd do it.

Piper stood up and snapped a few shots of the translucent turquoise ocean from the window while they waited. Who was joining them on the tour? There had been a few couples on the boat when she'd traveled on the ferry from Nassau, but she had been the only single person on board. Being the only single person present was the story of her life. By this point, she'd been on her own so much that she didn't know if she'd even function well in a relationship, whether she wanted one or not. Piper wasn't bitter about her continual single status. It was more like she was resigned to her fate because so far she'd not met a Dom who could accept a sub who only submitted in the bedroom, for reasons that she tended not to disclose to them. Piper had been steering her life for far too long and balked at the idea of handing the reins over to anyone else.

Feeling like she needed to get higher up, change the focus, and play with the light a bit so she could get one killer shot, she asked, "Is there roof access? I'd love to get an aerial shot."

Jared joined her back at the window and said, "There is, but it's tricky with the slope of the roof. Not to worry, though, I can have Cal take you up in the chopper if you want some photos from up above."

She almost tap-danced, seeing the shot in her mind, and enjoying the surge of adrenaline that came when she slipped into her creative mode. "That would be great."

At the click of the door handle, Piper glanced over her shoulder at the intrusion. Jared's office door opened, whereupon Mary, his secretary, a proper English woman and submissive in her mid-fifties, entered. Her small, compact form was adorned in tweed and her salt and pepper hair scraped back into a bun. But it was the athletically built man striding in behind the secretary who made every molecule in Piper's body roar to life.

She knew him. They'd crossed paths a time or two before. Master Theo Brown wore a suit the way some men wore a pair of jeans. It was like his body was perfectly sculpted to be adorned in expensive linens and silk. And today's tailored, form-fitting dark navy slacks and matching blazer only heightened his inherent masculine grace. His crisp, ivory linen shirt was open at his neck, displaying a hint of his sculpted physique beneath, and a few whirls of dark chest hair. This was the first time she'd ever seen him without a tie.

His intense cinnamon gaze caressed her form briefly, like a man selecting a fine bottle of wine, before he turned his attention to Jared.

"Theo, thanks for coming," Jared said, leaving her alone at the window as he crossed his office and met Theo in the middle. They shook hands and Piper, always the face behind the camera, couldn't help but snap a few photos. They wouldn't be for the brochure, but who could resist two powerfully built Masters in their prime looking better than any cover model?

"Not a problem, mate. I'm delighted I could help." Theo's deep gruff voice made Piper think of the finest brandy doused with honey, and her toes instinctually curled in her boots.

"Have you met, Piper Delaney? She will be joining us on the tour. Piper is photographing the island for me," Jared said, holding his arm out toward her, inviting her in to their manly Dom presence.

Theo's eyes whipped back to her, and he acknowledged her with a slight nod. She approached the tall duo but Jared's presence was eclipsed by Theo, with his thick head of dark hair, graying slightly at his temples, and inherently steadfast gaze. At first glance, he was everything an upper crust British man should be: starch in his collar, dressed to the nines, the dark stubble lining his square jaw expertly trimmed, and bored eyes. But upon closer inspection, as he firmly clasped her hand in his much larger one, she noted the banked fires in his interested gaze. The man wasn't aloof at all. Piper's skin sizzled where they touched, and when he lightly brushed the back of her hand with his startlingly soft lips, like he was a titled lord greeting a lady, she nearly burst into flames. Goosebumps broke out on her skin. Then he raised his gaze, with his full lips pressed against her hand, and she shivered.

Holy smokes!

Master Theo packed a walloping punch. He wasn't a cold fish at all and it did melty things to her insides. His fires burned hotter and gave the illusion that they didn't burn, which was crazy because she felt like she was going up in flames over his touch. He was like a blue flame that you believed at first to be cool, but which was actually hotter than the rest and would singe the flesh in record time. His eyes were all smoldering, banked fires and she almost wished he would do something outlandish, like nibble on the back of her hand while he had it pressed against his lips. It would give her an excuse to test and see if touching him would set the rest of her body on fire as well.

"Piper, it's lovely to see you again. You're well?" he said as he straightened, still holding her hand with his.

She cleared her throat and replied, "Yes, I am. And you, Sir?"

At her breathy reply, he smiled and her pulse rate spiked. It wasn't just the fact that in his eyes was a Master's knowledge of the effect he had on her sensibilities, but that when he smiled, like he was doing now, her mind went utterly blank. It made her feel like a cat wanting to rub up against his warmth. The way his full lips grinned with a wholly wicked tilt made Piper imagine he would wear an identical expression when he had a sub writhing beneath him.

"Better now. Glad to be joining you," he said, offering a bit of flattery.

"I hope you both don't mind if we get underway. I have appointments to attend this afternoon," Jared murmured, heading toward the door.

"Certainly. After you," Theo said.

Piper bowed her head out of respect as she passed, then held her head high. In all her thirty-nine years, she had never cowered, and as much as she recognized the Dom in each man, she wasn't a wallflower. Piper didn't do the submissive thing outside the bedroom. For most of her life, she'd tried that route and been miserable. She believed there was a point and age one reached where you stopped trying to be what everyone else wanted you to be, and decided to be yourself, with all your foibles and hang-ups. She no longer cared if she was too much for the many Doms who had been and gone in her life. Even after everything she had experienced, the lengths she had had to go to in order to heal, she'd always been too much for most people. But she'd reached an age where she no longer tried to make herself fit into an acceptable column.

"We can certainly add those protections, J, but let me get an assessment of the rest of the place. I think we can put more under one umbrella," Theo was saying.

"That's good. I also want to take care of my estate while you're here," Jared said as they strode toward the elevator.

Theo asked, "Are you sure you're ready to include your sub—"

"I want Naomi cared for, whether I'm here or not."

Piper half listened to Jared and Theo talk on the way down. From the sound of their conversation, Theo was utilizing his skills as a solicitor for both the island and for Jared. It was sweet that Jared wanted to look out for his sub like that. His accent thickened when he spoke about Naomi. She must be quite impressive to make a Dom like Jared come to heel. Piper couldn't wait to meet her.

Jared showed them through the club, lobby, and restaurant first. Piper snapped photos with her digital as they went. She'd come back with her Nikon, adjust the lighting in the room, and play with angles more. Jared explained some of the new expansions on the island, like the newly minted pizza parlor near the beach, and the outdoor venue for weddings and concerts that would begin construction in November. There were more features that would be added down the line, but without the physical structures available for her to photograph, she wasn't concerned with those. Oh, she'd include them with the ad copy on the brochure, for sure, but she was more concerned with cataloging everything that was currently on the island and needed to be shot, adding items to the ever-growing list she was creating in her brain.

She liked the feel of the place. All the futuristic and green technology was great, she was all for saving the planet, but there was also a flow to the architecture. Smooth, clean lines; airy walkways and hallways. The BDSM theme was there, in every piece of furniture, and the guests they passed along the way seemed to be enjoying it to the utmost, but it didn't appear gaudy or bordello-ish. Rather, it made her think of elegance and grandeur.

It was quite a feat. And one she believed she could use to help make him a brochure that would have patrons from *Allure*, *Underworld*, and *Cuffs and Spurs* banging on the door. Granted, she knew that the owners of those clubs had already cleared the way, but for this place to thrive, they'd have to have guests filling the resort regularly past the initial rush.

As they moved through the hotel, Piper was fully aware of Theo's presence near her. She tried to ignore him. But she couldn't seem to stop the resonance in his voice from tickling inside her chest as he spoke or how his scent, a carnal, dark spicy aftershave, drifted on the breeze and slammed into her senses with all the grace of a grenade to her system when they exited the elevator outside.

The man was a potent mixture of uptight, sophisticated Brit mixed with all the trappings of a Master. It was a heady and distracting combination. Piper made herself focus and note different places to shoot as Jared drove them in the golf cart. She'd have to get lost a bit with her cameras, go where there wasn't anyone around, and take photographs. The island was a gem, with a profusion of greenery and flowers. The lonely mountain peak, likely a dormant volcano, rose in waves and giant spears of slate-colored rock.

The two men were conversing as they ascended the mountain but Piper paid them no heed, more intent on the surroundings than her companions. She could feel herself slipping into that space where her creativity took over and she disappeared into her art.

At one of the tiny crested abutments, she said, "Stop."

"Everything okay, lass?" Jared asked as he slammed on the brakes and the cart came to a shuddering halt atop the abutment.

Before either Dom could stop her, Piper was on the move. Climbing out of the vehicle, she said over her shoulder, "Yes, I just need to get this shot. Give me a minute."

And she walked away, feeling both men's eyes on her back as she did so. But there was only one pair that stirred her with their cinnamon intensity. She directed her focus to getting the photo, climbing up on the padded horse and crouching into position.

The world fell away until all that was present were the shuttered clicks of her camera. Even her breaths became one with her art as she held still to capture the imagery.

Chapter 2

Bloody hell. Talk about a nice view.

A man had to admire a well-formed posterior. When it came attached to such a delectable package as Piper Delaney, her round butt clad in tight-fitting jean shorts, it almost made Theo swallow his tongue. It also made another part of his anatomy stand at attention. She perched her body—rather precariously—on the padded horse in the nearby scene station.

As a precaution, he exited the cart and walked toward her quietly, in case she slipped off the damn thing. They were situated at one of the highest points on the island. She was near enough to the ledge that, if she fell, she could seriously injure herself—or worse. As the solicitor for the island, Theo knew it was a lawsuit waiting to occur. At least that was what he told himself as he approached. If he was honest, Theo would say he was entranced by her. By the way her taut form was perfectly still as she leaned forward, camera anchored in her hands as she clicked away. It was totally at odds with the impact of her frenetic energy.

And the Master in him conjured up a few scenarios, utilizing the space in the station to maximize the potential pleasure. Putting the sexy as sin Piper as the star in his fantasy.

Jared had mentioned that Piper would be here this week. She was as devastatingly beautiful now as she had been at Declan's wedding. Other than a casual hello that night nearly a year ago, Theo had not had the chance to do more than give her a passing glance. So he hadn't been prepared for the unexpected flash of desire hitting his system when they'd shaken hands. Or the fact that he found himself wanting to remove the camera from her hands, bind her supple form to the horse she was currently perched on, and slake his lust on her body.

Theo was thankful his suit jacket hid the bulk of his erection. He moved a bit further, closer into her space as she shimmied toward the edge of the horse.

She shot a hand out and snarled, "Don't come any closer, damnit, you'll ruin my concentration."

Her words brought him up short. What the everlasting hell? Did she think she could talk to a Master like that without there being repercussions? His hands itched to tan her backside. Theo couldn't remember a submissive ever talking to him like he was dog shit on a new shoe. When it came to being a Dominant, he was a traditionalist. A submissive was to be respectful to a Dom at all times. If and when she wasn't, he was all for punishment. He'd been known over the years as a stickler for rules and discipline. As a solicitor, it was his job to be. It was no surprise that his love of law and order translated into his need to dominate. And Piper's ass was just begging for a few blistering swats that would show her who was in charge. He did not take kindly to a sub being so rude, ever.

"Keep that up and I will give you the spanking you so richly deserve," he snapped, his hands flexing near his belt buckle.

She shifted her face then, the wisps of her silver blonde hair moving in the breeze, and gave him a direct stare with a single golden brow raised in his direction. "As I'm here for work, you'll forgive me if I don't bow and scrape before you. And as for the spanking: touch me, and I'll break your thing off."

She slid off the horse with a bounce in her step. Piper didn't walk so much as sashay back to the cart, sliding her sunglasses back on and shielding her big baby blue eyes. Theo clenched his fists. Never before had he had a sub be so dismissive of him. His Dom nature seethed as he stalked back to the cart. She would pay for her remarks. He would see to it.

The woman ignored him entirely as he climbed inside the back seat. Didn't she realize she was all but begging him to discipline her sweet ass? It infuriated him that the thought of giving her the spanking she so richly deserved ignited a ball of potent lust inside his gut. Where the hell had this sudden need for the kitty cat with teeth come from?

Theo picked up his yellow legal pad and ball point pen from the seat beside him, taking notes as Jared drove, continuing the tour. The island was, without a doubt, a winner. When he had more time, and wasn't here solely for work-related purposes, he would make it a point to sample the delights. Theo would visit at a later date with his only goal being to do nothing but slake his hunger on all the available bounty. In fact, he would make it a point to come during match week this spring and see whether he could garner a more permanent relationship. That didn't mean he didn't plan to find a willing sub while he was here. It had been far too long since he'd indulged in the fairer sex. This haven for those in the BDSM lifestyle meant he wouldn't have to worry about his fifteen-year-old son showing up on his doorstep and inadvertently interrupting a scene.

It wasn't that Jacob couldn't handle the knowledge. He was a bright kid, and when the time was right, Theo had every intention of making sure his son understood the complexities of the lifestyle and made a choice on whether or not it was right for him. However, part of the stipulation with his ex-wife was that in order to maintain a relationship with his son, he had to keep his lifestyle choice hidden until Jacob was of legal age.

While taking a turn through the available sub pool on this trip did have its merits and was what Theo had intended on doing, it was the confounding woman on the seat before him who garnered most of his attention during the tour. She gasped and murmured at Jared, making him stop at almost every bloody turn so that she could, in her own words, 'Find this spot again,' making Theo gnash his teeth. What should have taken an hour took almost two and by the tour's end, he was basting in his own sweat.

At the main hotel, Jared handed the cart key to Piper and said, "Would you like me to get Sean or Michael to show you where your villa is, lass?"

"I think I can manage. We can reconvene in two days and go over what I have then," she replied, taking the key from him after a brief hug, and moving into the driver's seat. The woman certainly didn't act like any other submissive of Theo's acquaintance. Perhaps that explained his fascination with her—well, that and the fact that he owed her spectacular ass a thorough spanking.

"That's a plan then, lass. I will have Mary call you with the time for us to meet," Jared said, giving her a smile.

Piper gave Jared a cheeky grin and said, "As long as I get to meet Naomi."

"I'll have her set up lunch for us then." Jared gave her a slight nod then turned to Theo and asked, "Ready?"

"As always. Piper, a pleasure. I'm sure we'll see one another again," he all but promised. Because, the next time they crossed paths, he'd have her across his knee for her impudence.

She gave him a bemused glance, like she knew he wanted to punish her, and then she gave him a cocky grin and said, "Not to worry, big guy, it will be our little secret."

He heard her chuckle as she drove off and couldn't stop the

small smile from forming. Make no mistake, that little sub had just tossed an incendiary his way, and Theo was looking forward to paying her back in kind. His palms still itched to tan her backside and would do so at the first chance that presented itself.

"I'm ready," Theo said, adjusting his belt and suit jacket to cover up the near constant state of his erection.

"What was that all about?" Jared asked as they rode the elevator up to the top floor and headed to his office.

"Just a sub getting herself into trouble," Theo explained, and was surprised Jared didn't agree with him.

"Be careful with Piper, Theo. As long as I've known her, she's never performed a public scene. We have other available subs on the island who would likely suit you better," Jared said as they entered his office.

Wait, what? No public scenes? "Never? As in, not once?"

"Not that I'm aware of, and you know I tend to keep my ear to the ground regarding club members. She's been to every one of the DFC clubs and not once has she played openly. Tobias and the California group tend to watch after her, when she's home. Tobias said she comes and socializes at Dungeon Pleasures frequently but turns down every Dom who shows interest or asks her to do a scene. When Tobias pressed her, she said that she had her reasons and would cancel her membership before being forced into an arrangement that didn't suit her."

Instead of sending up red flags, the information made Theo inherently curious and interested in her story. He had always liked solving a puzzle. And Piper Delaney was the bee's knees of puzzles. Why was she not sharing herself at clubs? Was she celibate? Into women? Asexual? "No one knows, not even Declan? What do you make of it?"

"No, not even Declan. He was the one who told Tobias to back off, so he may know, but he's not sharing if he does. If I wasn't with my Naomi, Piper is a sub I would try to crack open. There's a hurt there, if you ask me, a fear. What exactly it is, I'm not entirely certain, and I don't know if she's willing to face it yet. Why? You interested?" Jared goaded him, good naturedly, of course.

Theo's blood simmered at the thought of making that one kneel before him and the myriad of ways in which he could discipline her sweet ass. He shook his head and said, "In giving her the fucking spanking she deserves for her impudence, yes. But that little kitty has some teeth, so no thank you."

"Why? Worried that she might try to bite your pecker off?" Jared asked as he sat at the head of the conference table.

"No. There's never been a sub I couldn't handle." Although that one just might give him a run for his money. The thought of having Piper bound naked before him, eager to please him and do his bidding, begging him for release, was sexy as hell and made his gut twist in desire.

"Good enough. Just don't piss her off and make her leave. I'm lucky enough that we have such an acclaimed photographer in the lifestyle. If we're going to keep this place away from the public eye, I don't want to be forced to hire an outsider."

"Understandable," Theo said, removing his suit jacket and hanging it over the back of his chair. The air conditioning in the room kicked on, the nearby vents blasting him with cool air, and he damn near sighed. He was unused to the higher temperatures, as London was quite a bit cooler this time of year. When it came to Piper, he had no intention of going near that little sub—other than to administer her punishment at the first opportunity and make her withdraw her claws a bit.

Theo preferred submissives who understood and knew their place: preferably on their backs with their legs spread and ready to receive him. Once today's business was completed, he had every intention of heading to the club in the evening and finding a willing sub. "Now, the island needs—"

"I'd actually like to start with my estate and my will. I want Naomi taken care of should anything happen to me." Jared handed him a thick file as they sat at the mahogany conference table.

Theo thumbed through the documents as Mary brought in a fresh pot of heavenly smelling coffee and cinnamon scones. He was surprised by what Jared wanted to put in his will.

"Are you sure about this, J? I realize you care for the sub, but this is quite a large sum. The property value alone is rather steep." It always concerned Theo when there were vast resources at stake. He'd been in the legal field for far too long and had seen more than his fair share of men swayed by a pretty face, only to have it end up in disaster—and court.

From his trouser pocket, Jared withdrew a small, two-inch, light blue box and flipped open the *Tiffany* lid. On a bed of white satin sat a glittering four-carat canary diamond, winking up at him in the light. Jared's face was composed as he said, "I'm sure, Theo. I want this in place this week and completed first. I'm proposing this week, but wanted these wheels in motion first before I do so."

"And if she says no?" Theo asked, ever practical when it came to estate dealings.

"Don't jinx me, man. She loves me, of that I'm certain. I may have to convince her to marry me, but I don't see my life without her in it. Even if it takes me years of whittling down her reserve, she will be my wife. I want her and any children we may have to be protected, even without the vows."

"Then let me be the first to say congratulations. Because of the size of the assets, it will likely take me through tomorrow to draw up the full draft," Theo explained. All the Masters in the DFC were falling in love and getting married, while he continued his descent into being a lonely old sod who hadn't felt sweet release from a willing sub in ages.

"That's not a problem, as long as the wheels are in motion, that's good enough for me. I have a few things I must see to around the island. Make use of my office as if it were your own.

Mary can get you anything you need, including lunch from the restaurant."

"Thanks, J, will do," Theo said, grateful that he could stay in the cool air and enjoy the amenities Jared extended his way. He began arranging the assets into a list on his legal pad.

"Oh, and what I just told you stays between us," Jared said, his hand on the door knob.

"As your solicitor, our entire discussion is private," Theo responded. Not that he was a social butterfly, anyway. More often than not, he was at home or the London office for Apex, and he'd never been one for gossiping. In fact, he worried that he was becoming a bit of a loner, what with his tendency to avoid social interaction at the club.

"Appreciate it," Jared said and left him to his own devices, exiting the office.

As the blessed quiet settled in around him, Theo rolled up his sleeves and worked. Facts, ledgers, accounts, drafting legal documents, were all second nature for him. Jared had a sizable estate, larger than Theo had realized at first glance. Getting the documents into an organized and comprehensible format took some time, longer than he'd anticipated. In fact, hours later, he was still at it with a crick in his neck that felt like the entire Manchester United team had whacked him across the shoulder.

The sun was setting on the horizon, the sky darkening to shades of cobalt and dark mauve as he exited Jared's office for the day. Since he had every intention of returning first thing tomorrow morning, he left his briefcase on the conference table. After dinner this evening, Theo planned to stop by the club and did not want to cart it with him. Each station came fully equipped with toys, lube, condoms—anything an enterprising Dom might require during a session—so he didn't need his goody bag. And Theo was determined to be balls deep in a willing sub.

With his stomach grumbling from the lack of sustenance,

Theo headed to Master's Pleasure. The restaurant was a five-star dining establishment that made him think of some of the finer London gentlemen's clubs. It was made for the enterprising Dom. Theo noted the hidden loops on the table as his waitress, Beth, a young submissive he likely had a good twenty years on, served him in her tiny costume: slicked on red leather shorts and a white bustier. Instead of inciting his lust with her pert globes smooshed against her top, she made Theo feel old with her small smile, and blushing countenance. The tanned brunette barely registered on his internal Richter scale.

It wasn't that she was not attractive or that he couldn't get himself into the mood if it were warranted. He could. Bloody hell, he was only forty-four. He wasn't dead. And he could certainly appreciate an attractive submissive, regardless of her age, but he preferred one with a bit more seasoning, one who wasn't quite so fresh-faced and nubile. A younger Dom might call him a daft old prick but as it was, he could barely muster appreciation for her charms. The chit had no fire in her that he could see.

Theo ate alone, preferring to study how the restaurant functioned than mingle with the other patrons. His chicken paillard was excellent. He would have to give his compliments to the chef. In his mind, he made a list of things to add to the island disclaimers, mainly due to the discipline scene occurring at one of the tables, four over from him. They had to make sure that visitors understood the risks of potentially combining food and bodily fluids—that while from all indications the wait staff thoroughly cleaned each station between guests, that did not mean something wouldn't be missed once in a while. It was all about safeguarding the island and the club from potential lawsuits. With people from other clubs like *Cuffs and Spurs* able to attend, it was Theo's opinion that they needed to make sure someone couldn't sue the island for damages if something untoward happened. That didn't mean something would, be he was a believer in being prepared for the worst. Theo knew Carter. His club was reputable, but things happened. Maybe they needed to have a stipulation on STD testing. They had one for the DFC club members, with requirements to get tested every six weeks. Perhaps that was a stipulation that needed to be included. He wasn't certain what type of regulations were in place at the other clubs.

Theo finished his dinner early enough that he felt a nightcap was warranted. Then he would head to his villa alone. After the lackluster interest he'd felt toward the waitress, he was no longer in the mood to entice a sub into his bed. And any time he did consider perhaps finding a sub to scene with and screw, the woman who came to mind was Piper, which was a rather peculiar development. Why that one? She had claws and teeth. Not to mention the fact that she did not act as if she had a submissive bone in her body.

What she did have was a killer body that stirred his lust in ways he hadn't felt in years, if ever. His cock hardened, straining against the confines of his slacks just thinking about her downright fuckable body. Unbelievable. The one sub he yearned to sink himself into was the one he wanted to stay as far away from as possible. What a bleeding shame his prick wanted that she-cat.

He rode the lift to the club level. The doors slid open with a ding and sound swamped him. The island club was a happening place, and packed with a profusion of people this evening. Heavy rock music pumped through hidden speakers in the walls. It pleased Theo that the temperature control was state of the art. It might be muggy and hotter than the fires of hell outside, but in here, it was comfortable enough for Doms to wear leather trousers. The subs, on the other hand, appeared to be wearing as little clothing as possible, with a few opting to go without a stitch. Theo appreciated the finer points of the lifestyle and the feminine flesh on display, but there wasn't a single submissive who stood out for him. With an eye toward the bar, he wove through the crowd, nodding at and greeting Doms he was acquainted with as he passed by.

At the glossy black bar, he said to the bartender, "Can I get a Macallan on the rocks, please?"

"Certainly. Jared mentioned you might be in and that I should make sure you were taken care of. I'm Sean, by the way, and am here most nights."

"You're the chef's son, aren't you?" Theo asked, seeing a resemblance to the woman he'd complimented on her extraordinary cooking not thirty minutes ago.

"One of them. My brother, Michael, is running around on the island somewhere as well. Here you are, on the house," Sean said, placing his drink on the bar.

"Appreciate it," Theo murmured, toasting the young bartender, and setting down a tip for him.

Taking a sip of the smooth whisky, he scanned the room. Theo liked the energy of the place with its muted lights, glossy black décor, and plenty of flesh on display. He didn't recognize many of the couples already engaged with each other in the scene alcoves. Then again, he knew club attendees were an eclectic mixture of employees and island guests. There was a particularly busty, brunette sub he thought he'd seen at the registration desk when he arrived, currently sandwiched between two of the boat captains and keening her head off as they screwed her brains out.

And then he spied her. Theo's entire being electrified and was instantly aroused. Piper hadn't changed her outfit and was still wearing the sodding denim shorts he had admired earlier for the way they cupped the taut, firm globes of her spectacular ass. Her flowery, turquoise tank top hugged her lean form, displaying her ample cleavage. Theo couldn't help but admire the athletic lines of her back, and the wealth of golden hair pulled into one of those messy buns at her nape, with shorter tendrils escaping and framing her face.

He had to adjust himself as his erection strained against the confines of his slacks. Christ, he wanted to bend her over and slake his lust on her body, claws and all.

The rules of the club stated that all submissives must be properly attired in club gear. Normally those same rules were enforced by the DMs, however, presently it appeared that all the DMs, except Jeff, were already engaged for the evening. If the DM wasn't going to do something about her apparel, as a Master, it was something Theo wouldn't let slide. She drew him as though they were attached by marionette strings. He had promised her retribution for her earlier snub. No self-respecting Dom would let those insults pass without administering punishment. And Theo didn't intend to, his hands itched to feel her lush ass beneath his palms.

He tossed back the remaining contents of his drink, the smooth burn of the Macallan as it slid into his belly making him smile. He was going to enjoy watching her squirm.

Theo maneuvered through the crowded room, his gaze intent on his prey as he strode over to her. Piper had her back to the room, ignoring the patrons and guests, snapping photos with a high-tech camera. The way she held the device, her camera was an extension of the woman herself as she filmed the vacant alcove that contained a padded, black leather sawhorse. Absolutely perfect for the punishment he had in mind for her sweet, delectable arse. Pleasure streamed through his body. He'd finally get a chance to touch her and growled low in his throat in delight at the thought.

Theo had to admit, Piper's ability to stand utterly still gave her a unique poise. When he neared her tight little body, her body heat emanated off her, stirring his lust and beckoning him closer. His cock strained, eager to sink into her body and see if she would set him ablaze. He growled into her ear and said, "It's against the rules for a sub not to be properly attired."

He took her momentary flinch as a reason to put his hands

on her. His fingers closed around her rigid biceps to hold her steady and keep her from escaping. She shot him a glance over her shoulder, her thick tresses escaping from their bun, teasing his chin, then she barely batted an eye and said, her voice dripping disdain, "Excuse me, Sir, but Jared gave me permission to photograph in here as I am. As the owner, I figure his orders carry more weight. If you will excuse me."

Piper tried to jerk her arms from his grasp but now that Theo had her, there was no way in hell he was releasing her. Not now that he could feel how silky smooth her skin was under his fingers, or the way she smelled like violets and rain, or that the condemnation in her baby blue gaze made a ball of lust slam into his solar plexus and damn near rattle his normally stalwart composure. Piper was the first challenge his Dom heart had experienced for an age, and it was intoxicating.

"No, I don't excuse you. And this is a domain where the laws are explicitly stated in the submissive packet." Theo was a sucker for rules. He admired law and order, and respected the system and belief that a society could only function with regulations in place for people to follow. That belief extended to how he comported himself as a Master. One didn't break the rules or they suffered consequences. In the case of a misbehaving submissive, it meant a firm spanking was in order.

She snorted, actually snorted in his face, the little termagant, then rolled her eyes and confessed, "I didn't read it."

Then she went back to attempting to wriggle from his hold, a kinetic sexual heat swirling between them. His raging hard on surged against the confines of his trousers. What did it, what pushed him over his limit, was the eye roll. This little sub would learn her place if he had anything to say about it. Not to mention that he'd been fantasizing about having her writhing beneath him all damn day, ever since he had spied her delectable rear on top of the horse that morning.

"You do realize you've earned this, love," Theo said, then

bodily carted her over to the sawhorse she'd just been photographing.

Piper went ballistic, like a feral she-cat about to be baptized as she railed against his hold. "Put me down, you stuffy, pig-headed buffoon. I didn't give you permission to—"

His rage seethed over her blatant disregard and he landed a firm swat on her ass. Then he snarled, "Silence. I did not give you permission to speak. You've earned this punishment. Now be a good girl and take it."

At the horse, they tussled for dominance. Theo was stronger and considered himself to be in the right, using his superior strength to cage her form against the furniture as she burned herself out. She struggled and bucked against him. Her firm ass wiggled and rubbed against his groin—not in invitation, but to unseat him. No matter her intent, the movement made his eyes cross and his dick strained against the confines of his slacks. He would take consummate pleasure in making this little sub come to heel.

In the end, Theo won, but just barely. Piper was a firecracker of energy and if she hadn't been holding her camera with one hand, she might have batted him away. It gave Theo the upper hand in their tug of war battle for the upper hand. He bound her waist to the sawhorse and the hand without the camera into a cuff, before he stripped the camera from her other hand, placing it on a nearby table, and fully restrained her body from the waist up.

It called to every dominant bone in his body seeing her bent over the horse and restrained. Bloody hell, it aroused him to maddening heights as his eyes caressed her form. Pure perfection.

"Son of a bitch, let me out of this," she protested, straining against her bonds to no avail. She kicked back with her feet, targeting his shins. One of her booted heels landed not so delicately on his calf.

"Cut it out, Piper. You earned this spanking and you fucking know it. Keep it up and I will ensure you don't sit pretty for days. Now, you will take your punishment like a good little submissive, understood?"

Theo yanked her shorts and panties down to her knees. He bit back a groan. Christ, the woman had a delicate little butterfly tattoo just above the taut globes of her rear. Her bottom cheeks were golden skinned and smoothly rounded. They would fill his hands nicely. Theo couldn't help himself, he traced his forefinger over the sexy tattoo. The woman had a naughty streak in her and damnit all to hell but he wanted to explore her depths, part the pretty globes and plunge his cock into her cunt. He imagined rubbing his crown against the tat, spreading pre-cum over it until it glistened up at him. Focusing on the colorful butterfly as he pounded inside her warmth.

He gritted his teeth at the storm of lust battering his system. Theo yearned to fuck the little sub with a ferocity that surprised him. It took every ounce of his control to stifle his desires and focus on the task at hand. He inhaled a few steadying breaths before he initiated her punishment.

Once he had his lust under control, he began, and did what he'd wanted to do all damn day long. Theo pulled his hand back, letting it fall with a loud crack against her bottom. He spanked her butt, not holding back, but laying into her rear with blistering strokes. As his swats tanned her hide, her golden skin pinkened beneath his touch. Satisfaction flowed through him, feeling the crack of her taut flesh beneath his hand.

Piper yelped, still struggling to break free of her bonds during the first few strokes of his palm as he thwacked against her bare bottom. But then she contained her cries as he continued with her discipline, emitting not more than a few mumbled oaths.

Theo was entranced, making sure his swats hit each of her finely-honed globes, and more turned on than he had been for an age. He could smell her arousal. It fueled his own, his dick surging against his pants, wanting to be set free, craving to slide inside her welcoming heat. Moisture glistened, seeping from her crease, and he nearly fell on her like a raving beast. It took everything inside him, every controlling measure he had in his Dom arsenal, to keep himself from undoing his pants and pounding away. That was not what this session was about. But it didn't stop him from wondering what her sweet cream tasted like, or how the warm heat of her pussy would feel clamped snugly around his dick.

He imagined it felt like heaven.

After thirty swats on her delectable rear, her ass glowed a becoming ruby red. Theo had sent her the message she needed to learn, that he would brook no rudeness or back talk the way he had today. Even though her punishment was done, he wasn't ready to release her from his control just yet. He yearned to continue touching her, yearned to do a hell of a lot more than just touch her. Instead of releasing her, he massaged the fiery globes of her delectable rear. He truly couldn't help himself, her supple backside beckoned his hands like beacons. When Piper didn't protest his caress, he grew bolder, and ran a finger through her dewy folds.

Bloody hell. He groaned internally; her pussy was drenched from his punishment. His fingers circled her nub, teasing her clit. A strangled moan erupted from her as he tormented her flesh, his strokes driving his desire higher.

Christ, he was nearly desperate to taste her cream, bury his face between her thighs and suck on her bud until she screamed her release. He was delighted by her response to his caress, but he wanted this little she-cat to beg for his touch. Then he would pleasure them both.

"Say the word, Piper, tell me what you want and I can give you the release your body is begging me for."

Her spine stiffened at his words and she snarled, "Let me go, Sir."

He almost smiled at her defiance. Two could play this game. Her body was so near release, she'd be miserable without an orgasm. She'd come to him, beg him to take her… when she was ready. In the meantime, he enjoyed watching her wriggle away from him as he undid her restraints.

She yanked her pants back on. A slight hiss escaped her lips. It was the only indication of her discomfort from his discipline. He wanted to applaud her stalwart performance.

"Piper, you let me know when you need me," he said, noting that her nipples were hard points beneath her top, and her breathing labored.

Her quixotic blue gaze whipped to his, full of self-righteous indignation, and he felt he was lucky she wasn't holding a weapon. "Hell will have frozen over, Sir," she said, and marched first out of arm's reach and then the club before he could stop her.

Theo didn't regret disciplining her sweet ass. On the contrary, he had enjoyed himself more tonight than he had in months.

Chapter 3

Damn the stuffy Brit.

Piper exited through the door leading out of the club at near Mach ten speeds and took the stairs down to the ground floor. The discipline had shaken her. Her anxiety level had skyrocketed at being forced into submission that way. She needed to take the anti-anxiety medication she had on standby as soon as she returned to the villa. It would be the only way she could stifle the rising panic. Piper hated that she was running away in defeat.

What she wanted to do was go on the attack and hurl anything she could find at that smug bastard's devilishly sexy head. Her bottom burned from his discipline. It had been years since she'd been spanked, what with her avoidance of clubs. The dratted man knew precisely how to strike for maximum impact. So much so that it felt like his large hand was imprinted on her behind. What gave him the right to spank her at will? It wasn't like he was her Dom.

Fury battled with her panic. She'd bring her grievance before Jared. The treatment she'd received at Theo's hands tonight had been unprovoked and uncalled for. Was she a submissive? Yes, she was, but only in the bedroom. Outside of there, she didn't submit—or bow and scrape—regardless of whether it offended a Dom or not. And if a Dom did feel slighted, that was his problem, not hers. Piper had not traveled to the island to be a Dom's plaything or submissive whipping post, but to do her job.

And that man, with his cultured British accent and huge hands, could go to hell. Piper drove her cart with fury riddling her body. She had stomped her way to the little vehicle rather than stick around to endure his smug expression. He'd known she had been turned on by the spanking, but had left her wanting rather than leaving her satisfied.

If there was one thing she would never do, it was beg—for anything. There had been one instance in her life where she had pleaded for mercy, begged for the pain to stop, only to have her screams and pleas fall on deaf ears. Fourteen years had passed since then and there were times, like now, where the public humiliation she experienced at Theo's hands dredged up the horrid memory.

Panic beat frenetically in her system, her chest tight to the point where she was close to hyper-ventilating. Son of a bitch, she couldn't breathe. Her hands shook on the steering wheel as she attempted a few deep, meditative breaths. Piper focused on drawing her breaths deep into her lungs and holding them there. It took her the entire drive back to the villa to corral her panic down to acceptable levels.

As she parked the cart, she angrily swiped at the wetness trailing over her cheeks. She hated the weakness, hated how something so simple as being publicly disciplined could make all their faces return in blistering, hills-are-alive, surround-sound detail.

Piper rode the elevator up and headed directly for her medication. She stood at the kitchen sink, in the state-of-the-art kitchen with its marble countertops, stainless steel appliances, and hardwood floors, and trembled as she struggled to open her prescription bottle. The Ativan was fast acting and would hit her system within twenty minutes or so, but to help herself in the meantime, she padded into the bathroom and headed directly into the shower. She had discovered years ago that showers, bubble baths and even, on occasion, relaxing in a hot tub, could help circumvent an attack before it was full blown as she waited for her medication to kick in. She stood directly under the hot spray. Anything to calm the fury-induced panic and burn away the vestiges of recalled horrors.

No one save her therapist, Dr. Caroline Winters, knew the extent of her situation. It was better that people didn't know. The last thing Piper wanted were the pitying glances or the knowing looks. It had taken her years to put herself back together after the attack. In the intervening years, she'd built an entirely new foundation for her life. Except she worried that, if anyone knew or discovered the lengths she'd had to go to to survive the rebuilding process, or how much of a handicap she walked around with, it would undermine the progress she'd made in her recovery. Granted, her therapist thought she was being defensive by refusing to open up to people about her attack. Which might well be the case, but just the fact that she could have sex and actually enjoy it was a feat of damn near mythic proportions. Other people didn't need to know about her sad little story. It was none of their business. And she didn't want to be looked at differently.

The attack was why she didn't play in clubs and couldn't perform public scenes. They were a recipe for a panic episode. Piper had tried, a few times, with an older Dom in Germany a few years ago, and discovered a hard truth. She was a defective submissive who couldn't submit outside the bedroom. A public scene unearthed her demons from that night. Her Dom at the time, Peter, had been patient and understanding with her, for the most part. He had done everything he was capable of to try and help her heal. But in the end, her dysfunctions were too much, so they had parted ways because he couldn't contend with a submissive who couldn't submit the way he needed.

And since that relationship, Piper had a few—and by few, she meant she could count them on one hand—one night stands, but none of them had been very satisfying.

Piper shut off the water, winced as the towel grazed her rear as she wrapped it around herself, and stepped from the shower. The man had not been gentle with his discipline in the slightest. She hated how good it had felt, that she had lost herself in his disciplined strokes for a time, and how all those demons that normally roared to the forefront in public had been blissfully silent.

Why Theo? Why had they gone silent for him?

It infuriated her, the conundrum he presented. She didn't want or need the distraction. She had her life in a set pattern. It may not be the most exciting or emotionally satisfying, but it worked for Piper. Her siblings were always attempting to set her up or give her advice because they assumed that since she was single, she must be miserable. When that wasn't it at all.

They didn't know the extent of her attack. They knew something had happened when she'd been on assignment in Africa all those years ago, that she'd become ill, but she'd kept the main details of the event, how near death she had come, from them. As the oldest sibling, it had always been her job to protect them, even from the harsh truth. And if she told them, they would worry every time she went on assignment. Piper couldn't live under a microscope, even for the sake of those she loved. She needed freedom to come and go as she pleased.

In her robe, with anxiety medicine humming in her veins and calming her enough that she could function, she sat at the kitchen table with her laptop and camera, uploading the shots she'd taken that day. Piper labored, sifting through the possibilities, burying herself in her work as she did, time and time again.

She worked until nearly midnight, when the medication nudged her toward sleep. On the bright side, her medication always helped her fall asleep quickly. But instead of the deep, restful sleep she expected, all night she dreamt of warm cinnamon eyes, tossing, and turning until she gave up the pretense of sleep in the early hour before dawn.

As she shuffled around the kitchen, the world outside her window sill at the darkest apex before dawn, Piper mainlined coffee like a heroin junkie getting their fix. She typically avoided taking the anxiety medicine unless absolutely necessary, since it tended to make her groggy the next day. While the caffeine worked its way into her system, she packed her backpack, stocking it with all the essentials she might need while tromping through the jungle, including her camera gear. As long as she was able to steer clear of any venomous snakes, she should be okay.

Piper left her villa before the first streaks of dawn illuminated the night sky. She veered off the lighted pathway into the dense forest. The island held all manner of life. Trudging through the brush as fingers of sunlight inched across the sky, she found an abutment that might make for one killer of a shot—if she could just get her gear set up quickly enough.

The villa next to hers had an uninterrupted east overlook view of the ocean that was stunning. She vaulted up the stairs to the deck and rushed to set up her equipment. It took her only a few minutes to erect her tripod and get her Nikon into position.

Piper started shooting as the sun's rays speared the horizon. The shuttering clicks of her camera filled the space, mingling with tweeting birds and buzzing insects as the world awakened for the day. It was magnificent. Part of the reason she loved what she did was getting a chance to witness the glory of nature.

She moved closer to the edge of the deck, taking her camera off the tripod and leaning against the railing. Magnificent. These shots were incredible, the colors alone with the vivid orange and pinks. She wished for her darkroom to develop the prints immediately.

"Would you mind telling me what the bloody hell you're doing on my deck?" a male voice said behind her. Only it wasn't any male voice. It was his. Theo. She could feel him directly behind her, and instead of unsettling her, like it should have, her body purred at his nearness.

"I'm photographing the ocean for Jared's island brochure, if you must know. It's why he hired me. The view from this deck was calling me, and I had to get the shot. I hadn't realized anyone was staying in this villa. I didn't mean to disturb you but I have a job to do. And Jared gave me his blessing, confirming that I had access to everything." She shrugged and finally moved, turning her head and glancing at him.

Holy hotness!

Looking decidedly rumpled, Theo's six-foot frame stood in a pair of green plaid pajama bottoms and nothing else but acres of finely honed muscle, covered with a smattering of dark hair coating his chest and arms. The man was sexy as hell and she'd have to be dead not to be attracted to his dark good looks. And last she checked, she still had a pulse. His dark hair hadn't been brushed yet and was messy, sticking out everywhere. It should have been unflattering. It wasn't. That, combined with his sinful mouth curved in a downward pout over her intrusion into his morning, shrouded by a day's worth of dark stubble, gave her the sudden urge to nibble on his plump lower lip and dry hump his leg. His enormous feet were bare and looking at their size, combined with his large hands, she wondered what might lie hidden under his pants. From the outline in his pajamas, he had been blessed and endowed.

Was it wrong that she wanted to find out?

"So you're not above trespassing and bothering other guests to get your shot?" he asked, placing his hands on his hips. For a split second, she wanted those big hands of his on her body.

"No, not really. Most of the island guests aren't even up yet, so I figured if anyone was around they wouldn't even know I was here. And now that I know it was you…" she said, feeling a perverse satisfaction that she might have ruined his morning.

"Now that you know it was me, what?" he said, a tick in his jaw as he glared, his cinnamon eyes burning with indignation.

Oh sweet heavens, Doms and their righteous fury over every little thing. If anyone needed to relax a bit, it was Theo.

"Take a chill pill, big guy. I didn't mean to disturb your morning ritual. I just," she shifted a bit, suddenly seeing a shot in her mind. "Forget what I said—would you mind if I got you in the shot? Could you pose at the deck railing, looking out over the water? I swear I won't get your face or anything, just your back, so no one will recognize that it's you."

Suspicion mingled with his stern Alpha Dom countenance and he asked, "Why? I thought Jared expressly forbid you from photographing guests. That, with the privacy constraints, guests were not to be filmed at all."

"Yes, I know what he said and I'm not trying to violate the rules. Besides, if you want to get technical, you're not a guest, either. But there's this shot I can see in my head and it's brilliant. Do me a solid, big guy, and pose for me. It will work, I will even give you a copy you can put in your home. And, to sweeten the pot, I will even give you final approval of the image before it ever sees the light of day."

"You want me just like this, without a shirt on, half nude in your photo?" He gestured to his chest.

She rolled her eyes in exasperation as the light she needed was fading. "Oh Jesus, stop being so damn British for just a second and do the shot. I promise it won't hurt. You might actually like it. And you could show it to all the subs in London who I'm sure will swoon over it."

"I'm long past the age where women swoon over me, love."

"No, you're not, but you just want the compliment too damn

badly. It's not like you need a boost to your ego. Will you do the damn shot or not? I don't have all day, man, we're going to lose the light here." Piper's temper was escalating into dangerous territory. She didn't know whether she would smack him upside the head or kiss him.

"On one condition," he said, his face an indecipherable mask.

"And that condition would be?" She prayed for patience, because if she prayed for strength, she'd use it to strangle him. Why him? Why had she been saddled with him as the thorn in her side on her stay here? Couldn't she have a nice, easy trip without being confronted with Master Uptight?

With a shuttered, incomprehensible expression, he said, "Submit to me while we are here this week. No strings attached, and we go our separate ways at the end of the week."

"What?" Piper wouldn't have been more surprised if he had morphed into the Loch Ness Monster. He wanted her, for the week, as his submissive? She would have believed the mystical creature bit more.

He shrugged his broad shoulders nonchalantly, but his eyes held banked embers in them. Then, giving her body a once over, his gaze stripping her on the spot, he asked, "Or are you not a submissive? It's a bleeding pity if you aren't, but even so, I'd like you in my bed this week."

Damn it all. His blatant proposal should infuriate her, except it didn't. In fact, it did the opposite. Her insides melted at the thought of granting him an all-access pass to basically screw her brains out. Instead of telling him to get bent over his outrageous proposition, she said, "I am a sub, but I don't think it's a good idea. I can pay you for the shot."

The thought of feeling his enormous hands on her body made her shiver, and not in disgust. Especially not after feeling his fingers toy with her sex last night. The problem with accepting his proposal was that he was a Master, and a rather traditional one to boot. Theo would expect obedience and submission in all things and areas—and that wasn't Piper.

Theo shook his head and said, "I don't want your money, love, but your body. Yes or no. My willingness to pose for you is losing its luster."

Damnit. She glanced at the rising sun and back at him.

"You already said you find me attractive. What's the harm, Piper? Take a risk. I promise to make it worth your while." He wasn't subtle and didn't try to seduce. No, he was honest about what he wanted, which was her. Unexpected excitement shot through her and her insides quivered.

Was losing her independence this week worth the shot? Could she submit to him? She wanted him, too, if the ooey-gooey melty sensations in her core were anything to go by. As independent as she had always been, the thought of submitting to his mastery and having sex with something that wasn't battery operated made her body come to life. Theo stirred her, and he was correct in his assumption that she considered him a walking wet dream. It left her with no choice in the matter and her heart sank in her chest. Keeping up the pretense that she was unaffected by his proposition, Piper rolled her eyes at him and said, "Fine, we can do the hanky panky. Now go stand at the railing with your back to me."

She ignored the victory in his blazing cinnamon gaze and the hint of a grin making his laugh lines stand out on his handsome face. If she contemplated what she had just agreed to, she'd more than likely have a panic attack and lose the shot altogether. Once he stood overlooking the landscape, she spent the next five minutes directing him, having him put his hands on the railing, in his pockets, one on the rail and one on his hip. And through it all, she wondered about the bargain she'd struck.

She told herself it was for the sake of her art. But deep down, she knew that was a lie. The thought of having him touch her again intimately made her insides quake, and not in terror but anticipation.

By the time the sun rose above the horizon, Piper knew it was going to be one hell of a shot. She only prayed it was worth the price she would pay.

Chapter 4

Theo's blood hummed in anticipation. She'd said yes. He would hold her to her word. At the myriad clicks of her camera behind him, he was thankful it was his back she was photographing and not his front. At her capitulation, the victory headed directly south, and his dick strained against the confines of his pajama pants.

He inhaled a few deep breaths to steady the sudden inferno of desire raging in his blood stream as he posed for Piper. She kept indicating he needed to relax. With her present, the kinetic sensual energy pull between them ignited his engines and turned them into smelting fires. Theo was a Master. He needed to dominate a woman, needed the control and utter surety that he would be obeyed—but Piper made him feel like an inexperienced twat, undermining his legendary control in club circles. That control was overridden by his desire, and the fact he found it difficult to keep his lust for her contained.

Bloody hell, but Theo wanted to pound himself inside her. Wrap her golden blonde tresses around his hand as he fucked them both senseless while gazing at her sexy tattoo. It should have made him feel like a cad, giving her an ultimatum the way he had for a bloody picture, except that part of his anatomy which craved the sweet clasp of her pussy didn't give a damn about formalities or niceties.

It had been so long since he'd had this magnitude of an awareness for a sub. Its potency was intoxicating. And now she had agreed to submit to his desires this week. He felt like a tiger about to pounce on its unsuspecting prey. As soon as their little impromptu photo shoot was done, he planned to do precisely that.

Sweet anticipation pulsed through his body. His hands curled into the deck railing as the clicks of her camera continued, forcing him to contain his rampant, raging need to fuck her.

"And that's a wrap. I'll let you see the photos and approve them before they go to print," she murmured, her focus already shifting from their interaction to her camera as he swiveled from his perch.

Finally!

Theo wasted no time. His body was primed and ready to sink into her body before he headed into the office. He'd tossed and turned thinking about her gorgeous ass all night long. Wondering what those firm globes would feel like in his hands as he slid himself inside her clasping heat. He needed her in his bed, her thighs spread and her body welcoming his. Once he'd slaked his thirst on her tight little body, then he might have a chance to focus on why he was here on the island.

He didn't ask for permission since she'd already given her consent to be his submissive this week, but hoisted her into his arms, heading directly toward his bed. He kicked the door shut behind him as he went, not bothering with a lock. They could go without all the trappings this first time. They would have time where he could bind her, and do the myriad number of scenes he'd fantasized about overnight. As it was, in this moment, Theo wanted her writhing and screaming his name beneath him and he wanted it now. His erection strained against his pants, aching to feel the taut clasp of her pussy surround his member.

"Wait just a damn minute," Piper screeched, struggling fruitlessly in his arms. Theo outweighed her and out-muscled her by a good seventy pounds.

He tossed her livewire body onto the mattress, his blood humming in anticipation of feeling her gorgeous curves undulating beneath him. Kneeling over her, Theo followed her onto the bed, but the little termagant crab-walked out from under him. Before he could restrain her with his form, the bloody sub scrambled to the other side of the bed and dismounted, putting the gulf of the mattress between them.

She held up her hands and took a few steps back from the bed, putting even more space between them. "Wait. Just what in the hell do you think you're doing?"

Theo's lust pulsed through his body. He couldn't believe she intended to play games. Rage seethed, combining with his arousal, and he snapped, "Are you daft? You agreed to be my sub for the week. I did as we agreed upon, now I want your pretty ass on my bed with your legs spread, ready to receive me."

"No," Piper said, planting her hands on her hips.

That did it. He vaulted off the mattress and stalked her around the bed. There was not a chance in hell he would let her renege on their bargain. Theo would tan her fucking hide first. He was the king of inventive punishments. Piper retreated as he advanced. He yanked her into his arms, caging her. She tried to push past him, but he was faster and stronger. He noticed the pulse at her throat thumping erratically as he backed her onto the mattress until she was wedged firmly beneath him. He was two hundred pounds of muscle. It would take a crane to move him.

He snarled, "You lied? The deal wasn't struck ten minutes ago and you've already reneged."

She rolled her eyes and said, "No, I didn't. I will submit to you, but I also have a job to do. Just because you're horny doesn't mean I'm going to fail at my job."

"I'm not suggesting that you do." That got his back up. She was acting like he was Cro-Magnon man, unable to control his lust and himself. And it hit remarkably too close to home for comfort. It enraged every dominant cell in his body.

"Dude, that's precisely what you're suggesting. You're horny and want to get laid. I can feel your erection. Great, that's why you have a hand. Just because I agreed to be with you this week does not supersede the fact that I have a life and work beyond this place that rests entirely on my ability to take pictures as needed, not as someone else dictates. I didn't build my business by chance or with someone else's handout. I did it on my own, there's a hustle involved where if you want to get to the top, you have to do what's necessary. I will submit, but it will be on my terms."

Piper words burned because she was right. He was so aroused by her that he wasn't acting like a Master at all. But that didn't diminish the fact that she had agreed to submit to him and then, the first time he required her submission, she tossed in a few amendments to their original bargain. As a Master, he wasn't used to compromise but to his word being law. He said, "And if I can't accept your terms, what then? I'm a Master, love, and everything you've just said makes me want to pull you over my knee and give you the spanking you so richly deserve."

A challenging light entered her eyes and she said, "Do it. I dare you."

Her small hands were pressed against his bare chest and felt like hot coals, branding him as she held him away from her lush body. She didn't cower or lower her eyes, but faced him head on. Daring him, calling on the very foundation of who he was as a Dominant and his desire to make the beautiful, unattainable wild wanton surrender to him.

However, if there was one thing he wouldn't stand for, it was a sub so blatantly waving a red flag in front of his face with her impudent cheekiness, goading him into punishing her. Before she could lobby a protest, he clasped her wrists in Velcro restraints and shifted her body until her beautiful ass lay over his thighs.

She bucked her hips, struggling against the restraints as he yanked her trousers down to her knees. Viewing the naked glory of the taut globes of her ass made him groan. Christ, but he wanted to nibble on her flesh. Unable to help himself, he kneaded her rear with one hand, grimacing in agony at the supple, smooth skin.

"When are you going to learn, love, that you can't speak that way to a Master and not face the consequences? You are forcing my hand here. No pun intended."

"Hardy har-har, you're a comedian. Let me up, dickwad. This isn't funny anymore." She attempted to wriggle her gorgeous butt off his lap but he wasn't having it. The woman had earned this spanking. And yeah, there was a part of him that was using it to put his hands on her, to sate part of his need to feel her beneath him. But he wouldn't allow himself to feel like a fool over it. He was a Dominant who had been without a sub for far too damn long.

He asked, a hint of a smile on his lips, "Dickwad, eh? Any more insults you want to add to the tally? May as well get it over with."

Piper was stronger than she appeared as she bucked, still fighting his hold, and she snarled, "Piss off."

This week was becoming a hell of a lot more interesting with her presence if the last twelve hours were anything to go by. He had every intention of exploring every facet of his interest in her this week. Leaning forward a bit, he pressed a forearm across her lower back, holding her in place, then drew his free hand back. Then he let his hand fall, putting power and force behind it. Theo wasn't a full-on sadist but he did appreciate a good discipline session. He walloped her rear, the smack cracking through the room. She screeched and mumbled something about biting his dick off, which drove him to land a few extra solid swats to her pretty butt, so hard it made his hand sting. Yet then she went still beneath him with only her gasps filling his ears. Theo concentrated on disciplining her, adding more swats at her verbal commentary.

She all but growled at him, her voice trembling as she said, "This isn't funny. You had your fun, now let me go."

He thwacked her butt thrice more, enjoying the way her supple form reddened beneath his touch.

"Son of a bitch, that hurt. I need to be able to move for my job, or do you plan on maiming me?"

"Keep it up, Piper. I could do this all day. And Jared would back me on this and you fucking know it, so give over, love. Hush now—unless you truly don't care whether you can sit at all."

"Stuffy fucking Brit."

"That I am," he replied and continued to pepper her taut behind. The tan globes deepened to a ruby red as his hand cracked across her backside. But she finally quieted down. It wasn't a surrender so much as a cease fire. Although, from her, he would take it, for now. It wasn't as if she was an easy nut to crack.

Her body was rigid beneath his touch. Granted, he wasn't being gentle in the slightest with his punishment. Piper needed to understand without a doubt that he would brook no disobedience from a submissive. She could fight him all she wanted; he would tame her, and her surrender would be the sweetest he had tasted in an age.

A trickle of wetness slicked her crease as his spanks slowed. She might be fighting it and him, but her body knew what it wanted. Theo finished her punishment, massaging the blazing red cheeks of her butt with one hand. He couldn't resist touching her slit. He bit back a groan at finding her drenched as he slid two fingers through her folds. He explored her, testing her body with his touch.

Her scent filled his nostrils as he played with her nub, circling it with his fingers as it swelled for him. He was indiscriminately pleased by her body's response. She wanted him. Even if she was rebelling, verbally at least, her body knew. A part of him which was still a mite bent out of shape over her rebuttal didn't want her torture to end just yet. He wanted her on her knees, begging him to fuck her.

Theo pressed two digits inside her weeping channel. Her pussy clasped at his fingers and he heard her indrawn, barely audible gasp. It drove him forward with his plan as he plundered her body with his hands. The feel of her slick heat grasping at his fingers drove his own desire higher and his erection strained to be freed, to sink into the warm sex his fingers were studiously thrusting into.

She contained her moans, still fighting his dominance, and it egged him on. She would scream his name, beg for his touch before their week was over. Theo added a third finger and Piper dropped her forehead onto the mattress. Her hips canted, meeting his penetrating thrusts, accepting him.

But she never said the words. She was magnificent in her pleasure. He couldn't remember ever being this aroused by a sub. He wanted to watch her ride him, wanted to replace his hand with his cock and hammer inside her pretty cunt until she had no choice but to surrender to his mastery.

Her body clenched and shuddered around his fingers, telling him without words that she was nearing orgasm. When she didn't ask him for what she wanted, he withdrew his hand. Needing to taste her essence, he sucked on his fingers coated with her cream, and damn near growled at her flavor. Christ, she was like the finest ambrosia. He'd spend an entire night just eating her. He undid her restraints, making it as clear as he could that he had no intention of going any further until she told him what she wanted.

She whimpered, her hips undulating on his lap. He tapped her rear.

"Tell me what you want, love."

She went rigid and before he could stop her, she scrambled away. She spilled onto the floor, hissing when her backside met the ground. Piper glared at him like an incensed goddess bent on man's destruction.

"I want you to stay away from me," she snapped.

"Not going to happen, or I tell Jared you welched on our bargain. You say you need this job. How kindly do you think Jared will take to your little stunt when he expressly forbade you from filming guests?"

She stood, yanking her shorts up, a slight wince being the only indication that the punishment had done anything to her.

As it was, he was having a remarkable time on the island. Much more so than he had originally believed he would. Theo said, "I expect you here, dressed and ready for dinner at six. We will attend the club after."

"I can't believe you're leaving me like this!" She gestured to her lower extremities with murder in her eyes.

He smiled, pleasure filling him at her distress. He was going to have an excellent time taming this little sub. He would cherish her surrender. "I only gift a sub with an orgasm when she behaves properly. And so far, you have not. Your frustration is your own doing. Submit freely without restraint and I promise you an orgasm that will make it worthwhile. Until then, I have a meeting in an hour, so cheerio. You can see yourself out."

Without a backward glance, he walked into the bathroom, heading into his shower, dropping his pajama bottoms on the way. He breathed a sigh of relief that his cock was no longer straining against the material, although the poor bastard would only have his hand to relieve him. But Theo left the bathroom door cracked open, just in case Piper decided to join him. If she did, he'd be balls deep inside her before she could speak.

Instead there was a loud thwack as she slammed out the back door of the villa and left. He laughed. She was an unexpected delight.

Chapter 5

*D*amn stuck up, snobby asshole.

Piper stomped away from Theo's lair fighting the need and desire coursing through her body. She whimpered as she strode through the jungle, carrying her equipment. With every step, her butt burned and her sex pulsed in anguish. She honestly didn't know which pain was worse.

The so-called agreement had been made in hell, to capture an image she didn't even know would be worth the trouble it had taken to get it. Especially since the blasted man apparently planned to torture her body into the heights of arousal, only to leave her unsatisfied and hanging in the breeze.

Damn Dom and his rules.

He was likely laughing his head off over her predicament. If it hadn't been for the impressive bulge pressed against her hip while he'd held her prisoner over his lap, she would have said he had been unaffected by her punishment and what happened afterward. Jesus, his fingers—those long, piano player ones—had almost made her climax the moment they slid inside her. In Piper's estimation and experience, most men were fairly easy. You showed a little tits and ass, and most were ready to do what you wanted them to. Except for Theo. The bastard had remarkable control.

His confidence that his orders would be followed to the letter and his obvious control over his urges were the marks of a true Master. Her face flamed with the indignity of her dilemma. Her nipples chafed against her bra, and just when she thought she had corralled her raging hormones down to an acceptable level, Piper would shift her legs a certain way through the brush and the ache would start again.

Damn him.

She tried focusing as she walked, searching the beautiful and picturesque island for those one in a million shots, angles, and moments to capture, but her senses were intricately tuned into the simmering desire he had ignited, and it all blurred together. The way he had stroked her, driving her body to the edge of blistering need, had awakened her body as if it had been slumbering. The discomfort was so intense, Piper finally caved midmorning. After fruitless attempts to make her body bend to her will and forget about Theo's long fingers as they had pumped inside her, she took matters into her own hands. On the west side of the island, she ventured into the deserted beach pleasure station, leaned against the far wall, and snaked a hand inside her shorts. After a few swipes against her swollen clit, pleasure burst inside her. She manually brought herself to orgasm twice more before she felt she could be reasonable and not want to kill the next person she ran into.

Once she was satisfied, and physically able to move without wanting to take a blunt object to Theo's head, she exited the station. With her camera and equipment, Piper trudged through the island, avoiding people, snapping shots wherever she found them. While she did feel marginally better, there was still a part of her that wanted to beg Theo to screw her brains out and give her the release only full penetration would accomplish. Her three climaxes had only dulled the edges of her sexual appetite.

How dare that man leave her so turned on? It was cruel and unusual punishment. What shocked her was how much she yearned for Theo. That stuffy dickwad of a Dom had made her crave his firm touch with just a few well-placed swats. Piper wasn't necessarily a sex kitten needing to get her load off every chance she got. She hadn't been since her attack.

But the mere thought of his hands thrusting inside her again made her sex walls clench and her body throb, begging for a release that only he could provide her. Why him? Of all the Doms in the world to turn her head, why that one? He was a stickler for rules and was far too uptight for her tastes. It didn't matter that his dominant control turned her insides into a melted marshmallow. Or that she craved his brand of dominance with a yearning she didn't fully comprehend. Frankly, it pissed her off. She didn't want to desire him. It was a wrinkle she didn't need in her life.

Piper arrived back at her villa late that afternoon, covered in grime and sweat from trampling through the forest. After she had showered, she immersed herself in her work for the next few hours. It was the one place that always made sense to her and where she was comfortable. There were days when it was like snuggling into a warm, comfortable blanket. It was familiar and safe. She used it to forget about Theo and his magnetic eyes that drew her into their cinnamon depths with merely a stern glance. The work she accomplished wasn't fruitless, and yielded better results than she would have guessed when she started. The photos she'd taken of Theo on the deck had been spot on and were fabulous. But seeing them, studying the lines of each image and making notes on how she wanted to expose the print to develop, which method she thought would be best, wasn't a cake walk. Her body responded to his image and it was difficult to ignore her craving for him. Today, she wasn't able to submerge herself in the job like normal.

That was her typical pattern when she was confronted with

anything resembling drama. Her therapist always commented that Piper was highly skilled at hiding herself in her work. And she couldn't deny that fact. Piper did it all the time, using her job as an escape from reality. Especially when she was in emotional turmoil and upheaval.

Theo was the king of monkey wrenches, disrupting her existence. Just because the man captivated her with his essence and dark good looks, made her insides quake and turn to jelly with a sinful glance, didn't mean she should lose her head over him. Theo was the epitome of the stiff-necked, traditional Dom. He would require submission in all areas, and all the accoutrements of convention that went with it. It was unfortunate because that was something Piper couldn't do. In another life, perhaps, but long ago she had let go of what might have been, of who she might have been, for the reality of what she had become through circumstance. Granting anyone her full submission wasn't possible for her. Piper wasn't built that way. She'd be lying if she tried.

Maybe if her attack had never happened, she'd be able to submit more freely. A part of her wanted it, wanted to give her worry, her fears, and everything that she was, over to the right Dom. But deep in her heart, anytime she contemplated handing her control over to another, inside she would seize up and freeze with a fear so deep and dark as to be the antithesis of light. Too much had been ripped from her soul that day fourteen years ago.

She'd spent a lifetime reclaiming her sense of self. If she gave herself fully, submitted to another completely, what would be left of her? The pieces of herself she had fought so hard to repossess belonged to her alone. Even the parts of herself that had died that day, as those men held her down and raped her one by one, laughing and grunting the whole time, those belonged to her.

There had been days initially following her gang rape when she had contemplated ending her own life. Days when she hadn't known whether she would make it to the next hour or minute, let alone the next day. But she'd persevered, and found the strength within to carry on. It had been her art that had saved her in the end. Not the thousands of hours of therapy, or the love of her family and friends, but her ability to sink herself into her creation. To just exist within it, look at life through camera lenses distantly and allow the inspiration to dominate her being.

So, in a way, Piper did surrender and submit, every day of her working life, but the difference was that it was her choice. The camera took nothing from her, expected nothing from her, didn't turn on her or cause her pain. It was safe. She had no problem trusting that it wouldn't hurt her. If it stopped functioning, she bought a new one. Plain, simple, and drama free, just as she liked it. Her art had been her salvation and what had brought her back from the brink of madness.

But Theo, that sexy as sin, inscrutable Dom, she feared wouldn't settle until he had claimed pieces of her soul. While she prized herself on holding true to her word, in this instance, she doubted her capitulation to their agreement would be wise.

Perhaps the best course of action would be if she circumvented their relationship, cutting it off at the knees before anything had a chance to develop. That way no one would be disappointed. She'd had enough of that rather fun emotion in her lifetime. And yes, she was playing it safe, but she knew firsthand the staggeringly steep cost when you didn't.

Besides, if that man thought she would appear on his doorstep at six like a little puppy dog he had trained, he had another thing coming. Piper was not in any way, shape, or form the obedient, simpering, wait-by-the-phone-for-your-command type of submissive female. It defied every ingrained part of her existence. She adored submitting in the bedroom. In fact, she could even do restraints now without freaking out and having an episode. Not to mention, she enjoyed the pain of a good caning or whipping. But as soon as she was outside of the bedroom, that all went away.

When her stomach growled, she pulled herself away from her computer and notes to cook dinner, forgoing the main hotel and restaurant entirely. Yes, she was avoiding running into Theo—or interaction with other humans for that matter—but she enjoyed a simple life, and the stillness and quiet that came hand in hand with being on her own. One thing Jared had done for her was stock her fridge. When she had mentioned needing to be alone to work for the majority of her time here, he had made sure she had a copiously supplied kitchen with everything she wanted to eat while on the island. Cooking was another joy for Piper, even if she was quite modest when it came to her meals. Tonight, she whipped up a quick chicken stir fry, loaded with veggies and some brown rice. She paired it with a rather large glass of Chardonnay.

Temperatures had cooled since the afternoon and Piper ventured outside to eat her dinner on the deck. There was a gentle breeze, the sun shining down as it made its descent for the evening. It almost reminded her of home. She ate meals on her patio there frequently. As she reclined on the deck on a chaise longue, munching on a flavorful bite with water chestnuts, she spotted a gorgeous little Woodstar who decided to stop by for a visit and perched itself on the deck rail. The size of a small robin, the bird was unique because of the bright coloring on its neck below the beak that was a vibrant, fuchsia purple. Piper was never far from a camera, and withdrew her small portable digital from her pocket.

"Well, aren't you just the prettiest thing," she murmured sweetly to it. The bird seemed to know she was talking to it and almost preened for her camera. She loved snapping wildlife. Anyone who thought they were dumb animals just didn't get it. She could see the beauty in the little beast's soul. And frankly, on most days, she far preferred animals over humans.

Her half-finished meal was forgotten as she took a series of shots. The bird even had a friend stop by to see what the fuss was about as she set up her tripod and larger Nikon to snap more photos of the two. Their playful antics on the deck railing as they chirped at one another brought a smile to her face. This was why she did what she did. She didn't pay attention to the time and immersed herself in catching the light as it faded.

Heavy footsteps clomped up the wooden deck stairs. It alarmed her bird friends and they zipped off, flying into the deepening green of the forest, and disappeared from her sight. Piper sighed to herself as Theo's powerful form joined her on the deck. She didn't look at him. She could feel the displeasure radiating off him. Instead of confronting the issue head on, she continued snapping images of nature around them as he invaded her personal space. While she didn't want to confront him, she wouldn't run from him either. She'd learned to stand her ground and face her fears.

"Forgive me if I'm wrong, but I seem to remember requesting your presence at my villa at six sharp." His stuffy British accent was thick with disapproval. There was no reason not to be straight with him. She owed him that at least for the photos this morning. The rest, she couldn't agree to. It was just too damn risky. Maybe if he hadn't been a sadist and left her in such painful need earlier, she might feel differently. She ignored the warning in his voice. As it was, she was rather peeved herself.

"I decided to decline your request. This arrangement is not going to work for me," she said, not bothering to glance in his direction. It really was better this way, for both of them.

"Did you now?" he replied, his voice deadly silent and rather dispassionate, which should have tipped her off.

Wind rushed across her face and suddenly his muscled shoulder dug into her stomach. The air whooshed from her lungs as he hoisted her in his arms. Stunned at having her world upended, she gasped for air as he carted her into her villa. For a stuffy Brit, he moved with a panther-like grace, and faster than she had time to recover from being turned upside-down. Before

Piper could utter a protest, Theo had stripped her and had her wrists fastened into cuffs on the St. Andrew's Cross in her private dungeon, putting her body on complete lockdown.

As if waking from her stupor, she struggled against her bonds and snapped at the dark head bent before her as he finished restraining her ankle, "Let me go this instant. My other camera is outside. It will be damaged if it's left out like that. You can't do this to me."

Theo gave her a succinct glance from his kneeling position, then said, "Wait here."

She sputtered and growled at his retreating back. How dare he do this to her? If that man thought she would submit to him now, or ever, he could forget about it. Piper wanted to tear his eyes out for this. Whatever deal he thought they had, was done. It didn't matter that a part of her yearned for his touch. That she admired his tall form as he retreated from the room, or that his confidence in his movements stirred her. He didn't waste his energy.

In less than two minutes, he waltzed back inside, hauling her tripod and Nikon. Piper breathed a deep sigh of relief that her equipment was safe, at least. Although, she didn't know how she would fare once Theo had finished with her, and she couldn't stop the tremors of fear riddling her system. Probably more discipline, from the stern look on his face. But would she survive the night with her soul intact?

"There, your camera is safe. Now we can focus on the fact that you have disobeyed every one of my requests since agreeing to our bargain. I will not accept any more stalling from you. It's time for you to start submitting," Theo said after he placed the camera down in the living room. He strode toward her, unbuttoning his dress shirt. And sweet Jesus, but the man was ripped. He wasn't the body builder type, but had the solid muscle of a man who had taken care of his body his entire life and was athletically inclined. There was a nice pelt of dark hair coating his chest, funneling into a single line over his smooth, six-pack stomach, and disappearing beneath his black trousers.

She snorted, but her body sang with pulse-pounding desire as he neared. With his outrageous actions, he forced her to confront her desire, the yearning he had ignited with his touch. By all that she was, Piper couldn't fathom turning away from him or from the way he made her feel. Then again, Theo hadn't left her much choice in the matter. As much as she tried to make herself not desire him, she couldn't lie, she did—and what's more, he knew it. The heady, dark expression on his face would brook no further delay on her part.

She inhaled a shaky breath. He would make her stick with her commitment and the bargain they had struck. That knowledge, that he would make her capitulate and succumb to his passionate demands, bend her will until she no longer desired to turn him away, made her bones all but liquefy and her blood simmer in expectation. Maybe she would finally have that orgasm she'd been denied.

"Fine. Have it your way," she conceded, cursing how breathy her voice sounded.

Theo flashed her a sensual grin and it was as if the sun finally shone on her for the first time. He twisted her insides into gooey mush. "Relax, I'm not going to hurt you, much, but I do plan to take you."

They were only words but combined with his potent erotic charisma, they made her sex flutter and lava enter her veins. Theo invaded her space on the cross until every masculine inch of him was pressing against her, leaving her no doubt as to his carnal intent. He cupped her chin, rubbing his thumb over her bottom lip. With his blatant hunger, his cinnamon gaze shifted to a dark molten bronze that she found herself drowning within. Piper didn't know what he was waiting for as he stared at her. Now that the decision was out of her hands, she craved his touch.

He asked, "What's your safeword?"

"Red."

"Good call," he murmured. Then his lips finally claimed hers, but it wasn't the invasion she assumed it would be. And it was that much more devastating in its simplicity. He explored her mouth like he was committing its shape and feel to his memory. And he was in complete, utter control. She moaned in the back of her throat as his tongue slid along hers, curling around hers, teasing her with delicate, playful thrusts. It was only when Piper surrendered, stopped trying to maneuver him and control the tenor of their exchange, that he changed the temperament of their kiss and ravaged her with torrid, deep caresses. Going deeper, he slid his hands into her hair, gripping her head to hold her steady as he plundered her mouth.

Piper's head swam. Carried by the tidal wave of his passion, she was drowning in him and his carnal kiss. In the way he drank her startled moans, demanding more from her, and with each stroke of his tongue, she gave it to him without question. Theo invaded the very fabric of her being.

It was only a kiss.

Yet every single part of Piper's body was affected by his caress. It was as if, with only a kiss, he managed to touch the very essence of her being. It was the most intimate and carnal embrace she'd ever experienced. Theo ran his hand from her wrists, restrained up above her head on the cross, down over her forearms and biceps, then on to her shoulders and the slope of her chest. He cupped her breasts in his large hands, rolling the nipples between his fingers and she mewled into his mouth. His caress veered over her ribcage, his hands grazed her abdomen and hips, but he avoided the juncture between her thighs.

At her whimper of frustration, he chuckled darkly but took the unending kiss even deeper. It made her forget her frustration as she kissed him back with equal ardor. Piper didn't want him to stop kissing her, ever.

How had he disarmed her entirely with merely a kiss? And did it really matter, when all she could see, could feel, and all she wanted, was him?

When her head fell back against her shoulders, only then did Theo pull away.

"There now, that wasn't so hard," he murmured seductively, giving her body a once over.

She watched him from her hooded gaze as he walked over to the armoire and began pulling items from it. Her belly quivered when she spied the riding crop. The man really was a sadist. But instead of making her squeamish, it aroused her beyond the pale. He fit the crop beneath his left arm as he returned to her.

"Now, I need you to use your safeword if you must, as this is our first real dalliance together and I don't know how much pain you can take. I will push your boundaries this week, but I also don't intend to cause you true and lasting damage. Understood?"

"Yes, Sir."

He gave her another grin, a white slash of teeth and devilish gleam in his eyes, before he bent forward and surrounded one of her nipples with his mouth. Unexpected pleasure pulsed as he laved the taut bud, pressing a series of sharp bites around it. He played with her nipple, teasing, and fondling the sensitive skin as it swelled at his touch. Pleasure raced along her veins as his tongue swirled and embraced her flesh.

This wasn't so bad. At present, with her body floating on a sea of passion, she couldn't remember why she'd thought being with Theo was a bad idea. Her eyes almost crossed when he tugged at her breast. The man's mouth was a little slice of heaven. Her world centered on the attention he lavished on the globe. Then he slid a cool metal ring around the engorged bud and tightened the four screws until the clamp was securely fastened. The four screws with blunt, smooth edges pinched and compressed her nipple. She hissed at the burning pressure.

"There now, that looks beautiful on you," Theo said, his

voice husky. His passionate regard flicked to her face, as if contemplating his next action, before he switched his attention to her other breast, giving it the same devotion as he had its twin. By the time he had affixed the ring of fire clamp around her second nipple, wetness was dribbling between her thighs. Theo aroused her body to maddening heights and, judging by the erotic countenance on his face, their night had only begun.

He stood back, admiring his handiwork as he stripped his dress shirt off entirely. She wanted to nibble on his broad shoulders, trace his powerfully built biceps with her tongue and explore his body like he was her own personal playground. Then he removed his black leather belt, and she bit her lip in anticipation of finally seeing the impressive bulge in his trousers. But the blasted man was toying with her and kept his black slacks on. Without the belt, they rode low on his hips, exposing his firm victory lines and the black band of his briefs. Sweet heavens, but Piper wanted to taste his victory lines with a vengeance.

Theo approached her, no longer looking like a stuffy Brit but every inch a Master, and her belly quivered as he tapped the leather crop against his palm. He said, "I'm going to test you and see how much pain you can take. Again, Piper, and this is important, if at any time something hurts too much, I need you to stop being bloody minded for a minute and use your fucking safeword."

She nodded, biting her lower lip. "Yes, Sir."

Like a whispered caress, Theo traced the riding crop over her body. The smooth leather grazed her throbbing nipples, teased the underside of her breasts, stroked down over her abdomen, and caressed the folds of her sex and inner thighs to her calves. Then he moved around to her back, brushing the exposed parts of flesh not hidden by the cross. He started along her shoulders, rubbed the silky leather down her sides to her rear. The leather traced her slit, teasing her with a hard stroke from her clitoris all the way to her rosette.

"Oh," she gasped, unable to keep her moan contained.

But her moan twisted into a surprised yelp as the crop landed on the fleshy part of her butt. Her nipples stabbed forward and painfully swelled against the rings of fire clamps, but the ache morphed into the sweetest pleasure imaginable. Piper eagerly anticipated the next swat. Theo didn't disappoint as he tested her body's response. The loud thwacks of the leather connecting with her flesh filled the villa.

He struck her ass with strong whacks. Piper had never necessarily considered herself a pain slut, but because of the way with which Theo handled the crop, the stinging force behind his lash, she was beginning to re-evaluate herself and her needs. He blistered her butt until she could feel the fiery burn which seemed to have a direct line to her pussy. Theo moved his skillful branding to her shoulders until they were engulfed in flames.

Then he moved back into her line of sight with an intense, deeply sensual expression clouding his gaze. His engorged cock strained against the confines of his slacks and Piper couldn't remember the last time she'd hungered for a Dom this much. She wanted him to fill her. She wanted him to fuck her. She wanted him. Then his hand snapped and the crop cracked against her swollen nipple. Lightning arced from her tit all the way to her pussy.

"Ah," she keened as yummy pleasure-pain spliced her nerve endings in lacerating waves.

Theo turned her breasts into a molten mass of acute ecstasy so intense she strained for his touch, whimpering with each blow against her stiff nipples. And then he thwacked the leather against the exterior of her pussy. Moisture flowed between her legs as her head dropped back.

"Oh god," she wailed at the scorching fire erupting in her veins. Piper's body existed in a sea of rosy joy.

At the swipe of his tongue through her pussy, she groaned. She was beyond feeling anything but the pleasure he offered her.

The man had one hell of a talented tongue as he caressed under her hood, laving her folds, spreading her plump pussy lips further apart and teasing her clitoris with his tongue and teeth. Theo didn't eat her pussy so much as he devoured her flesh like a man feasting on a buffet. He lapped at her cream. Curled his tongue around her engorged nub. Compressed his tongue against her bud, and then plunged inside her quivering channel. Pleasure spiraled and swelled as he seemed to know exactly where and how to touch her for maximum effect. If she could have moved, she would have, as her pleasure built with every thrust of his talented tongue. Except she could do nothing but surrender. Piper willingly flung her stalwart control away, all her defenses crumbling into the nearby ocean as she gave herself over to him and his care. She was past the point of reason and thought.

Piper moaned as he continued stroking her flesh. Her pleasure spiked to maddening heights. Her nipples stabbed almost too painfully now in the clamps. But she rode the bombarding waves of ecstasy as her body drew tighter in on itself with every drive of his tongue inside her trembling heat.

She wanted more, wanted to feel his cock thrusting inside her, yearning for it, for him to strip away his trousers and plunge his erection inside her quivering channel, but she said nothing. She moaned, she whimpered as he tortured her in the most pleasurable way possible, but she didn't ask him for what she wanted most. Then he removed his mouth from her pussy.

"Oh," she wailed. She glanced down her body to where he was kneeling between her thighs. Her cream glistened on his succulent lips and the stubble lining his chin, his breathing was labored, but it was the carnal hunger in his heavy-lidded gaze that rocked her to her core.

He seemed to be waiting on her, but still she said nothing. So he rose up to his full height before her and undid his slacks. He shucked his boxers and the full brunt of his desire bobbed before her gaze. Long, with a smooth head, his cock swayed, jutting with moisture glistening on his ruddy crown.

God, she wanted to feel him inside her. She wanted to taste him. She licked her lips, and he gazed at her with a raised brow. She knew what he wanted. Why she didn't say the words, she wasn't certain. He sheathed his cock, covering his length with a condom, but still he waited to penetrate her. Piper's body was on fire and she was so near climax from his skilled tongue that one thrust would likely send her body over the ledge.

Instead of screwing her brains out, Theo leaned down and swiped his tongue against an engorged nipple, massaging the flesh around the abused bud. Then he loosened the clamp and sucked the throbbing bud into his mouth. Flames shot from her breast to her pussy and she moaned. He laved and suckled her breast until there seemed to be a direct line from her tit to her clit.

Theo wanted to torture her, drive her crazy with his touch. When he moved his mouth to her other breast, his fingers teased her pussy, grazing her clit as he removed the second clamp. Piper tossed her head back and wailed in frustration. Her body was strung out and so over-sensitized by his attentions, she was near tears.

"Just tell me what you want, love, and I promise to give you what you need. You just have to say the words," he growled around her nipple and then bit down painfully. A raw lance of pleasure-pain blasted her system.

She screeched, "Please let me come, Sir, please fuck me."

"About fucking time," he said through gritted teeth.

She watched him as he gripped his bulging erection, rubbing the smooth head through her pussy lips until his member was positioned at her entrance. Her sex throbbed, ready to feel him inside her.

"Look at me, Piper," he ordered.

She lifted her gaze until all she saw was his molten bronze

one. At her compliance, he thrust, plunging his length inside her until his balls were pressed against her butt. Her body welcomed his and nearly came undone. She mewled. Her tissues stretched at the fullness of him, the way he strained inside her, her body clasping at his cock, trying to draw him deeper. Theo gripped her hips, his hands steady as he rolled his pelvis, pumping his shaft in and out, establishing a languid pace. After everything, the fact that he was lazily fucking her when what she wanted was hard, fast, and damn near brutal, was enough to drive her to madness.

Theo, the sadistic bastard that he was, seemed to know it, and grinned. "Not yet, love, you've done brilliantly, but you're still trying to control things."

His mouth descended, claiming her lips in a torrid kiss as he continued to thrust. He surrounded her on the cross, pressing his body against hers until she could no longer tell where she ended and he began. It was the kiss that did it. Theo knew precisely how to kiss her and make her head spin. Piper melted into him, past the point of reason or logic. She could feel her body as it tightened in on itself and she surrendered.

Theo was so tuned into her, the moment she ceded her power over to him, the cant of his thrusts changed. He never released her lips, thrusting his tongue inside her mouth in time with his cock pounding inside her weeping channel. Piper keened against his lips at the power behind his thrusts, harder, faster, but not once did he lose control.

He broke the kiss and growled, "Come for me."

He slammed home, his balls slapped against her rear, and her body erupted. "Oh god!" She screamed, her head falling back as she wailed. Starbursts exploded inside her body as he increased his tempo, his erection swelling as he plunged fervently.

But the man was a freaking machine. Piper was awash in pleasure as he pounded. Her body gripped his shaft as he plunged. Over and over, he hammered his cock inside her with such brutal precision, it was like he was imprinting himself on her body, branding her pussy as his. Spread as she was on the cross, all her decisions removed from her, she could do nothing but accept the violent storm of his lovemaking. Piper strained against the straps as he shuttled his cock in pounding digs. Her legs shook in their bonds as desire and pleasure became her entire existence. It boiled down to her and Theo, and his glorious cock pumping harder and faster.

Piper's body devolved and she was grunting as he pounded inside her flesh. The sounds she made were almost inhuman as her pleasure morphed into a state of ecstasy so pronounced, she could feel her body spinning out of control, reaching for an incredible peak that was so bright and pure, it burned with the fury of a thousand suns.

"Piper," he bellowed, pounding his member inside her with such force, another climax shattered her system so that she was blind to everything as her body imploded.

"Ah, Sir," she wailed.

Theo's cock thudded and he strained as his release swamped him. But eventually his thrusts slowed. His face was buried in the crook of her neck, his lips pressed against her skin. She kissed his neck, liking the stubbly feel of his shadow beard.

And then he lifted his soulful gaze up to hers, his eyes searching her face. Theo kissed her then with such tenderness, his hands cupping her face as if to say she was precious to him. Her world spun on its axis as she returned his kiss. She had no words for what had occurred between them. It had been unlike anything she'd ever experienced.

Piper didn't say anything as he released her lips and began undoing her restraints. He gently cleaned her body off with a towel, wiping the excess fluids from her and disposing of his condom. She wobbled on her feet as he helped her down from the cross. She didn't want to break the spell. Harsh reality would return soon enough. For tonight, she wanted the belonging, the comfort.

So she didn't fight it when her body sagged against his from overuse, or when he hefted her into his arms and carried her over to her bed. She didn't refuse him when he joined her there, spooned her in his arms, and settled into sleep. For tonight, having his big male body surrounding her with his strength, with his protection, was something she let herself enjoy without a thought as to why she shouldn't.

Piper slid into sleep with the thought that the stuffy Brit wasn't so stuffy after all.

And then she dropped like a stone over a ledge into oblivion.

Chapter 6

S unlight streaming across his face woke Theo up from a deep and dreamless sleep. He'd experienced an undisturbed slumber that was mainly due to the wonderful bounty of Piper's body last night. What a gobsmacking revelation she had been on the cross. It had been by far and away the best orgasm he'd had in years. Just remembering the way her pussy had clasped his knob made him hard again.

It also made him want a repeat performance, which was something he hadn't desired from a sub in years. Normally, once he'd tasted a woman's bounty and satisfied his own need to dominate, he moved on. It wasn't like he was able to have a normal Dom/sub relationship with his son living a stone's throw away from him.

Speaking of repeats... Theo reached for Piper's compact body only to encounter empty space and cold sheets.

He cracked an eye open. The room was empty. No problem, she was likely just in the loo or kitchen. Theo sat up in bed and said, "Piper?"

Nothing. He was alone, in her bed, with a raging hard-on, feeling like a right fool.

Bloody hell!

He left the bed and padded around her villa, double checking she wasn't outside on the deck shooting a leaf or tree or whatever the hell it was she did shoot. As he assessed her lodge, he noted that her camera equipment—the large tan backpack she'd been lugging around yesterday morning—was absent as well. It was as he suspected: she'd headed out and not told him. Normally he was a fairly level-headed bloke, or at least, he thought he wasn't a complete tosser, but the level of disrespect she'd shown him after he believed they had made some inroads last night stirred his anger.

She'd not even had the decency to leave him a note. As his intended sub for the week, he expected her to show a certain amount of decorum. Theo slid his trousers and shoes on, not bothering with his shirt, and left her villa. He tromped the short distance between their villas, swatting at gnats and feeling his temperature rise with his animosity. When he got his hands on her, he'd ensure that she understood her behavior was unacceptable and tan her sodding arse ruby red.

At his place, he showered and chugged down some coffee. Normally he preferred tea, but he wished to be tense until the matter with Piper was settled, so coffee it was. As he dressed for the self-imposed hike, he shot off a text message to Jared that he would be late into the office. He dressed in his long running shorts and tank top, with sneakers. No bloody way was he hiking through the scorching jungle to locate a misbehaving sub in a pair of trousers and dress shirt.

Theo simmered as he hiked through the forest and the island searching for Piper. He enjoyed the outdoors. He and his son did a bit of hiking up in the Scottish Highlands every year. Theo enjoyed the outdoors full stop, and the island was a beautiful tropical paradise that was also hotter than the fires of hell today. The sun beat down on his shoulders, sweat poured down his body, plastering his shirt to his chest, and the deeper he ventured into the island, the more resolute he became when it came to Piper.

He would discipline her sweet ass and they would come to terms. Maybe he should just leave her alone but after tasting her last night, he knew that once was not nearly enough. He wanted more, wanted to spend a full day in bed just figuring out what made her body tick.

As he neared the mountain, he discovered a crevice in the rocks no more than ten feet wide, hidden by brush and palm trees. If he wasn't so intent on finding Piper, he might have missed it. The crevice ran for a good thirty feet or more before it opened up at the other side. What he found stunned him into silence. It was a grotto of sorts. Jared had mentioned that there was a private body of water, fed by the ocean but enclosed on every side, save one. At the opposite end was a break in the mountain rocks, a small archway big enough that a small boat could sail through it. This was probably where Nick and Patrick parked their boat when they weren't out on assignment.

But the beauty of the place, the crystal-clear turquoise water, surrounded by a pristine white sand beach encircled by a profusion of greenery and slate rock walls, was a stunning sight to behold. It was as if Theo had conjured her up, the slim silhouette standing at her tripod, taking pictures. She reminded him of a mermaid washed ashore with her long, golden blonde hair, golden-toned skin that was softer than cashmere, wearing a form-fitting sky-blue tank top and skimpy tan shorts, displaying her toned legs. He wanted to remove the offending garments. That woman should always have her ass bare, at least in his presence. He still had yet to take her from behind, but was adding it to his already extensive list.

This little sub needed to understand who was boss.

Without further ado, Theo strode the rest of the way with a single-minded determination that, before either of them left this grotto, they would come to terms with their arrangement. Five feet from the golden beauty, he snarled, "Why didn't you wake me?"

She shot him an unconcerned glance over her shoulder and said, "Hello to you, too. Because it was five in the morning. And I had a feeling you wouldn't let me leave."

Then she all but dismissed him and went back to taking pictures. Was he that easy to get rid of? Theo had thought he'd made a bit more of an impression on her last night. He'd had subs a plenty in London and Scotland vying for a place in his bed. While his ex-wife might say he was a bit dull generally, she had never forgotten their aerobatics between the sheets.

"You're right about that," he snapped, trying not to sound as mardy as he felt.

"See, so you didn't leave me a choice in the matter. It really shouldn't be a surprise. And it was worth it, I've gotten some spectacular shots that I cannot wait to view once they're developed."

"Piper, that doesn't excuse the fact that you agreed to be my sub this week. Your behavior this morning was not how a sub properly behaves. Before we leave this grotto, I'm going to make sure you understand that it will not be tolerated."

He advanced, closing the distance between them with his intent clear on his face. But then Piper's face went ghost white and her body went from fluid to ramrod rigid before she screeched, "Like hell, dickwad!" And then she took off, sprinting down the beach, away from him like he was a sea creature bent on making her his next meal.

Christ, what game is she playing at now?

Theo raced after her, pursuing his prey with determination. She would understand that for this week, he was her Master. But she didn't need to fear him. Her reaction made no sense. This wasn't the Piper he'd come to know. Then again, how much did he really know about her?

PIPER'S HEART pounded wildly in her chest as she sprinted across the sand. Dread clawed up her throat, strangling the breath from her lungs. She repeated where she was, who she was, and who it was that was chasing her. Anxiety and fear overshadowed her movements and were making it difficult to remember. She wouldn't allow Theo to punish her for doing her job. She didn't deserve it. This was precisely why she thought an arrangement between them was a terrible idea.

Fear has a funny way of sneaking past your defenses at the most inopportune instances. As she ran across the secluded, unspoiled beach that had brought her such peaceful joy moments ago, it dissolved and transformed before her eyes to Serengeti grasslands. Violent laughter and horrid grunts from memories long ago roared in her ears as an episode clamored into her psyche and battled to take hold.

Not now. I can't lose control. Not when I need to get away.

But there was no stopping the freight train of the panic attack as it washed over her system like a tsunami. The sights, the sounds, the sharp agony—all of it came rushing back with the force of a grenade to her system and she stumbled along the beach, not seeing the beach at all but the savannah, and a motley group of men with evil in their eyes. She didn't hear Theo. He wasn't in her memories. Only wicked men, howling in delight as they took their turn. Her legs pumped over the sand as she ran, blind to everything but her past.

A firm, muscled hand wrapped around her bicep from behind. Piper screamed bloody murder. They were going to hurt her again, make her beg them to stop, make her wish she would just die already to make the pain stop. She stumbled as she tried to wrench herself away as the past overshadowed everything. She fought him—them—using her fists, she beat against his chest. Piper kicked, she punched, she forgot her self-defense training as her panic overrode every logical thought process in her full-on attack. She couldn't see the surrounding beach but was back on that grassy plain with a camp fire smoking heavily nearby. Dark faces hovered over her. The slapping of flesh and her shrieks pierced the night as they hooted and grunted.

It was the last bit that zapped her ability to fight. She caved, wanting it over, wanting to feel relief and peace. She curled into a ball, turning inward where there was no pain. The horrid men didn't exist there. Tears streamed unheeded down her face, blinding her vision.

"Piper, Piper. Please talk to me, sweetheart. It's okay. I'm not going to hurt you.

"Come on, sweetie, it's okay. Piper, can you hear me, love? Say something, anything…

"Piper, I've got you. Nothing's going to happen to you. Talk to me." Theo's deep bass, laced with concern, finally broke through her terror. His strong arms circled her as he gently rocked her on his lap. One of his big hands tenderly stroked down her back in a calming, soothing rhythm.

"Piper, can you hear me? Talk to me, love. What just happened?" Theo's craggy, handsome face hovered over hers. It was like seeing sunlight after being in a darkened room for days. She used the naked worry in his cinnamon eyes as an anchor to pull herself out of the quagmire of her nightmare.

As the past receded and the bright light of day entered her field of vision, she realized that she'd had an attack. It was the first one she had experienced in almost a year, probably because she'd let her defenses down last night. That was one of the main reasons why she usually kept her emotions firmly in check, controlling how much she allowed in or out. It made her panic attacks easier to control and she could go for longer periods between occurrences.

Shame filled her—that she'd let Theo witness an occurrence. She hated being viewed as weak or helpless.

"I'm sorry. You can put me down now. Please, I promise I'm okay. I'm sorry that you had to see that," Piper said in a rush, when what she wanted was to escape his steady gaze and lick her wounds in private. She hated people seeing her like this, even her therapist, whom she had known for more than a decade.

Theo shook his head, his stare fixed on her, and said, "No. I'm not letting you up until you talk to me. What happened?"

She closed her eyes, moisture still seeping from them. She had been crying and not even realized it. This had been a bad one. Maybe it was because she was so twisted up by Theo and their session, and she was so tired all the time from working too much. Except, she couldn't erase the fact that it had occurred or that Theo had witnessed it. What she could do was take steps to ensure she didn't have another one, since they tended to come in threes. As for explaining her attack to Theo, she didn't want to go there. It was why she had avoided relationships with Doms in the first place, keeping her interactions to a one-night thing, because they always wanted to fix a sub. The problem was, there were some hurts that went far too deep, and no matter how much time passed, this wound would never fully heal.

"I can't. Please, just let me go, Sir," she pleaded with him, not caring that she had to resort to begging.

One of Theo's dark brows rose as he contemplated her and said, "It's not going to happen, love, so you may as well give up. Tell me what just happened, why did you go nuclear?"

She winced when she spied angry red gouges in his chest peeking above his tank top. They were the size and breadth of her fingernails. She'd done that: hurt him—not much, but she had left marks on him and the damage had been done. And the sad part was she didn't remember physically doing it. When her attacks were that bad, she didn't even know where she was anymore.

She looked down at her hands. Her cuticles really needed a

trim. Then she inhaled a deep breath and said, "I'm sorry. I had a panic attack. I get them from time to time."

"What precipitates the attacks? Maybe it's something I can help you with this week."

She shook her head. That was the last thing she wanted. She had to end this with him, now, before he dug too deep. She pleaded with him, "Theo, don't, please. Don't go looking to be a white knight and try to save me from myself. This isn't something that will go away in a week, or a year, or ever. I'm sorry that you had to see it, but it's best for all concerned if you leave me alone."

"Like hell. Piper, even if I didn't want you, I would still not leave you to your own devices after seeing that. I wouldn't leave anyone suffering."

Which was why she kept her distance. She'd tried the whole Dom attempting to fix her routine and it had failed spectacularly. Piper knew the best course of action on her part was to withdraw and retreat. "But you can't fix me. Nothing can. Just trust me on this, and let me go."

"Not a chance. Besides, how do you know if you don't try?" Theo was so earnest in his belief, it made a part of her want to trust him with her darkest horror, to lay it at his feet, and let him go all super Dom on her.

She laughed then, a bitter, sharp bark even to her ears. Who the hell was she kidding? There was no hope for it and she snapped, "What do you even know about it, with your cushy life and 'I'm a big bad Dom' attitude? I'll tell you. You know nothing about me. I've been trying to get over it for fourteen damn years. Do you really think that I haven't tried that already?"

"Don't think you know me either, Piper. You think my life is easy or cushy? I've watched another man help raise my son with my ex-wife. Donald's a decent enough bloke, but Jacob is my son. Do you think for a second that's been easy, or 'cushy,' as you say it? Fuck no, it hasn't, but at least I asked for help. So it didn't work the first time around. Big deal."

"And you don't think I haven't tried? Theo, I have a therapist on speed dial. These panic attacks are not new and they aren't going away. I can control them, keep a lid on them if I... never mind what I have to do to control them. It's not your problem, just please leave it be and let me go."

He shook his head, his face hard as granite, and she knew deep down he wasn't going to let her off the hook that easily. He said, "No. Not until I get some answers. Why did the panic attack happen just now? What triggered it, so I can know not to do it in the future? And why do you have them, what do they stem from? You owe me that at least, since I will be walking around with your claw marks for the remainder of the week."

"I'm truly sorry about those. I didn't know I was doing it. Let's just say I was in the wrong place at the wrong time, and bad things happened. Things you don't just get over—if ever—and ever since that event, I've had panic attacks. It's why I don't do public scenes, ever. I had one just now because of last night," she explained, needing him to understand that their little arrangement had to come to an end.

His arms stiffened and he glared, his eyes going cold as he asked, "What do you mean, because of last night?"

"Because I submitted to you completely. It opened the doorway I normally keep contained and likely dredged it up." Guilt swamped her. She wasn't blaming him, but she had to make him walk away. It was the only way she'd get her peace of mind back.

Theo's hand tilted her face up toward his and he held her steady. "Then we are going to have to work on that this week. And I will help you. You can't keep yourself in an emotionless box for the rest of your life, Piper. You have to open up to someone."

That's where he was wrong. She explained, her breaths shuddering out of her lungs, "It hurts me more if I do. I can't be who or what you want me to be. I just don't have that in me. Maybe I did once, but that woman died fourteen years ago and she's not coming back."

He stroked her cheek tenderly with his thumb. "It's also a lonely way to live."

It was, she couldn't deny that fact. Except, she was used to being on her own and not counting on anyone. She'd been alone for so long, it was the only method of existence she was familiar with anymore. Piper attempted to downplay the truth of his words, unwilling to display just how much her single status did bother her and how broken it made her feel. So she shrugged and said, "But it works for me. Why rock the boat?"

"Because the woman who came undone under my hands last night deserves to exist with as much passion for living as she does her photography," he murmured, his eyes softer, with a wealth of meaning in their depths that made her belly clench.

Piper looked at him then, really looked at him. Theo hadn't dumped her in the sand and walked away when she was embroiled in her episode. Instead, he'd offered comfort and soothed her, bringing her back from the darkness inside. He'd heard a neutered version of her attack and hadn't batted an eye. Was he strong enough to know the whole truth? Could she clasp at the tiny tendril of hope and open the door for more? She was so tired of being on her own all the time. As much as she professed to be okay with her single status, she wasn't, not really. It was an act on her part, because she hated being portrayed as a victim and didn't want other people's pity. When, in truth, she yearned for a firm shoulder to lean on once in a while, when the weight of her world grew too heavy for her to carry on her own. And he surprised her with his steadfast sense of honor in not leaving her while she was freaking out on him. She wasn't used to people sticking by her—other than those she'd paid to do so.

Her heart shivered. Going on instinct alone, she erased the

distance separating them and brushed her lips against his. Theo saw her like no one else did. No Dom had ever said she had passion. Most thought she was a cold fish, and incapable of the most basic human responses. How or why Theo could see her for who she was, and did not condemn her because she wasn't this paragon of submissive virtue, caused warmth to spread in her chest.

Then Piper kissed him, sucking his bottom lip into her mouth, tracing its form. His stubble scraped deliciously against her flesh, causing goosebumps to break out over her skin. She knew some women didn't care for beards or five o'clock shadows, decrying that they were uncomfortable. But she adored the rough texture against her skin. Piper outlined his mouth, seeking entrance, wanting—nay, needing—to show him how much it meant to her that he hadn't left her when it mattered most. She wasn't ready to examine her feelings, but she could show him her appreciation and submit to him. It was only when she caressed his tongue, tangling it in a heady duel with hers, that Theo made his move, like he had been waiting to discover how far she would go first before he assumed control of their make-out session.

And then Theo kissed her as if his life depended upon it.

He held her, cradled within his arms, on a secluded beach, and kissed her like no man ever had before. As if she mattered. It was an intoxicating and altogether new experience for Piper. Maybe it was the fact that he knew a bit about her attack, and a bond forged with him, forming as he kissed her senseless.

It terrified her.

Piper feared depending upon someone who would eventually leave her, discard her once they learned the full extent of her traumatic experience. Just as she was about to withdraw and break their connection, one of Theo's sinful hands undid the button clasp on her shorts and snaked beneath the linen material, delving beneath her panties to her sex. Two of his long fingers caressed her pussy, fondling her clitoris. Her eyes closed as pleasure sparked at his touch. The digits circling her nub teased and cajoled her body into heightened awareness. It was as if Piper's body had been chemically calibrated to respond to Theo. Desire pulsed through her veins as he stroked her sensitive flesh. She moaned into his mouth when he nipped her bottom lip, leaving her with no doubt as to his intensions.

With everything that had occurred this morning, she conceded, opening her legs wider and granting him access. He growled into her mouth as he plundered deeper while his fingers caressed her folds. Then he penetrated her quivering channel with two digits, pushing forward until they were embedded deep within, her walls clasping at him. His thumb circled her clitoris, pressing against the bud as his fingers began to rhythmically pump inside her.

She canted her hips, meeting his sweltering thrusts, and gave herself over into his hands. Literally. Each roll of her hips sparked embers of pleasure that speared her system. Her body became intricately tuned to Theo's, grasping at his fingers, trying to pull him deeper inside, and she never stopped kissing him. Telling him with more than words that she appreciated how he'd brought her back down from her panicked state, and how much she wanted him.

Theo was relentless as he stoked her passionate flames higher, adding a third and then a fourth finger, stretching her sheath as he plunged. Over and over, he thrust, driving her body toward a blistering climax. She writhed, riding his hand as scorching flames incinerated her being, her core tightening in on itself as the blaze grew hotter.

Piper jolted, her pussy flooding with moisture as a fireworks display erupted inside her body, and she clenched and shuddered around his thrusting fingers as her climax hit. She moaned into his mouth as wave upon wave of pleasure overflowed and she trembled with the force of it. Theo didn't remove his hand until the pulsations in her sheath diminished. Then he withdrew his digits from her apex. Her eyes fluttered open when he lifted his mouth from hers. He lifted his hand, coated with her dew, and swallowed the fingers into his mouth, his tongue licking up all her cream and tasting her essence.

Riveted by his actions, lust encapsulated her. Theo's erotic nature was attuned with her energy. His actions stirred her, and even though she'd just had an orgasm, she craved more of his loving. Maybe it was an escape she sought. A brief chance to erase the horrible morning memories of her panic attack. But she didn't care what the reasoning was or whether it would bite her in the ass later. She wanted him.

"Thank you for telling me." He shifted her off his lap to her feet and then stood, donning his lawyer-esque, bland, boring façade. Theo gave her a slight nod, dismissing her like she was nothing more than a secretary and said, "I will let you get back to your work."

If it weren't for the bulge in his shorts and the banked embers in his eyes, she'd have said he was an eunuch to have brought her to climax and then walk away without a thought for getting off himself.

Like hell he was leaving. She said, gesturing toward his crotch, "No, clearly we aren't done yet."

"Piper, don't worry about me. We will reconvene this evening. I have work to see to."

Now he was the one shutting her down and it scared her. He had already put four feet between them when she scrambled up to her feet. Was he worried that he had tangled with the crazy woman? She couldn't let him leave here like this, and did the first thing that popped into her head. She stripped. Her tank top and bra landed in the sand at her feet, followed a swift second later by her shorts and panties.

She never took her eyes off him. The distance he'd attempted to erect dropped away as each garment hit the sand. The embers in his eyes shifted, turning into hungry, dark flames. It was her turn to entice him, draw him out of his shell. Maybe that was why they seemed to mesh so well. In all those spiritual self-help books she'd studied as she'd worked toward healing herself internally, they always mentioned that like recognized like, like attracted like. So perhaps Theo was a bit of an island himself, just like her.

Piper held out her hand, waiting for him to make a move, one way or another. Her breath caught in her throat. If he turned away from her now, after everything, it would be worse than if he'd run while she'd had her attack. On the edge of anxiety, she wondered if it would be the tipping point that would make her shatter if he walked.

Theo appeared to have an internal debate with himself that lasted a minute or more. It felt like a lifetime. But then he reached for the hem of his shirt and nearly tore off the offending garment. His shorts followed. The man took her breath away. Tall, muscled, with his erection jutting proudly, his powerful thighs and calves dusted with fine, dark hair. Absolutely mouthwatering. Piper's body was electrified by his nude form.

Only then did Theo approach her. His hand closed around her smaller one, and he towed her into the surf until they were waist deep. Then he pulled her into the circle of his arms, his hands stroking down her back until they cupped her butt. His erection pressed into her belly. Every place their bodies touched became electrified. Her body molded itself to his. She was more than ready for him, to feel the weight of his cock pound away inside her. Sliding her arms around his neck and hoisting her legs around his waist, Piper wrapped her body around his. It fit his length along her apex and pleasure speared her. This was her choice. He was her choice as she rubbed her sex against his member.

Theo groaned at her antics, his hips thrusting against her ministrations. Then he moaned. "Bloody hell, I don't have any protection, love, we might need to—"

"I can't get pregnant, if that's what you're concerned about. We don't need it." There wasn't any chance in hell she was letting him get away from her. She couldn't have kids and was clean. All members in their club were routinely tested for STDs, so that wasn't a concern.

"Are you certain?" he asked, his eyes searching hers for confirmation.

Instead of a verbal response, as an answer, Piper reached between their bodies, grasped his shaft, lifted her hips, and fit the head of his erection at her opening. Then she thrust her hips down. Theo groaned, his grip on her ass cheeks tightened, and he dug his fingers in as he held her, fully embedded in her channel.

"Good enough," he murmured and then rolled his hips. Piper kept her eyes open and trained on his as they moved together. Folded around his body like she was a second skin, accepting his unforgiving thrusts, grinding her hips, they established a wild rhythm. And all the while, she never took her eyes off him.

He did likewise, holding her close, digging his hands into her rear. And the rest of the world receded. It was like they were the only two people on the planet in their very own Garden of Eden. Desire rose unbidden and unhindered. Theo thrust harder, faster, ramming his cock in brutal digs. Piper writhed, canting her hips and meeting his ardent plunges. He filled her, stretching the walls of her pussy as he drove himself inside her.

Their moans joined the cacophony of birds and insects, filling their private grotto with the sounds of their lovemaking. Through it all, they never broke eye contact. With every hammered stroke, Piper felt an organ she had long denied crack open wider. As much as she wanted their lovemaking to continue, she could feel the edges of her climax building, pleasure raining through her body. He pulled her tighter, like he was attempting to crawl inside her and make them one being, clasping her against his chest as his thrusts became animalistic. Piper ground her hips, meeting his ramming plunges. He grunted and groaned as he hammered his hips.

He buried his face in her neck as desire eclipsed everything else.

"Theo!" She keened as her body toppled over the edge and she came apart at the seams. Pleasure ricocheted in cosmic bursts of world-altering sonic booms. She vibrated in his arms, ecstasy pumping through her veins.

"Piper," Theo bellowed. His cock jerked within her buttery folds, jets of hot cum jettisoned inside her trembling depths, setting off a secondary round of sparks. She held on to Theo for dear life as her body trembled and soared. His movements slowed as his body emptied a full stream of semen inside her quaking channel.

Theo just held her then, with the sunlight beating down upon their heads, the cool ocean water lapping at their waists, and their heart rates returning to normal. Tears formed in her eyes. When was the last time she'd been cuddled this way after sex? As much as she feared it, because of what it made her open up, she craved the intimacy, the repleteness and comfort of just being held. She sniffed her tears back, not wanting him to think she was having another episode. His tender care was making her go all maudlin. If she wasn't careful she'd start building castles in the sky, and hoping for something that just wasn't to be. Yet she couldn't seem to tear herself away from him. In fact, she was still plastered around his form like a second skin.

Theo shifted, tugging her face up to his. He searched her face, his molten gaze turning her insides into mushy goo. He brought one of his hands up to her cheek, stroking it with his knuckles before he kissed her tenderly.

Her heart, that muscle she'd worked for years to protect and keep from anyone, quaked as she returned his kiss. Theo released her lips, still cradling her cheek, and said, "Meet me for dinner, tonight at six at Master's Pleasure."

"I don't know," Piper deflected, at war with herself over how to proceed with Theo.

"That's not a request. It's just dinner. You know, the thing two people do when they are dating," he said, giving her a sexy grin.

"We are?"

"Aren't we? I think we've passed the point of denying there's something between us. It's just dinner, Piper. Come on, take a chance, experience a bit of what life has to offer. What do you have to lose?"

Everything.

But he was so earnest in his desire to have a meal with her in public, like a date, that she couldn't refuse him, "Okay, fine. I will meet you there at six."

"That's a girl," he murmured, giving her a quick buss on the lips before finally withdrawing from her body. He set her on her feet, and then towed her out of the water with him.

She let him help her dress, getting to witness a playful, relaxed Theo, who smiled more in those ten minutes than she'd seen him do the entire time she'd known him. Piper became filled with purpose by witnessing what her capitulation and surrender had engendered in him. It was quite the transformation. Gone was the stodgy lawyer and in his place was a kind, playful man she, wonder of wonders, wanted to get to know more.

He kissed her again before he left her alone on the secluded beach, giving her a love tap on her butt as he left with a, 'be there or else,' Dom order that made her toes curl.

What did she have to lose at dinner tonight?

Only her heart.

Chapter 7

Throughout the day Piper told herself she was being a fool. That she should disregard Theo, ignore her budding feelings for him, and cancel the purported date.

Except she didn't want to.

Piper had been in the dating desert for what seemed like eons. She could count on one hand the number of instances where she'd been asked to dinner with an attractive man. On that handful of dates, not one man had twisted her insides into silly putty with merely a glance. The thought of turning Theo down and not going on their date tonight was unfathomable. It would elevate their relationship from only physical into more, as if they were, in fact, dating. Even with the bargain they had struck, it went beyond the parameters of their arrangement.

Then there was the man of the hour himself. The sex—oh my goodness—she pressed a hand against her midsection just thinking about that morning and her entire body melted into a massive puddle of sexual delirium. He made her weak-kneed and made her burn. If she wasn't careful, he would become an addiction more potent than any drug or alcohol.

In the last twenty-four hours, she'd orgasmed more than she had in the past month, thanks to Theo and his lovemaking. And she wanted more, craved his sinful touch. There was a part of Piper that yearned for the intimacy of a real Dominant and submissive relationship. And Theo was the first Dom in all these years to whom she'd ever wanted to unburden her sorrows and hurts. Even if there was no way to fix her broken pieces, it would be wonderful to just have someone she could turn to when the weight of them became too much for her to carry the load on her own.

Piper cut her day of shooting short to prepare for their date. Perhaps she was placing too much importance on it, but when you existed in the dating wasteland, going years between dates, it tended to be significant when you had one. She lounged in a bubble bath, of all things, shaved her legs, and pampered her skin with a sugar scrub and moisturizer until it glowed. With a few well-placed pins, she artfully arranged her hair into a stylish up-do at her nape. That way her enterprising Dom could remove them easily and her hair would cascade down her back. She shivered at the thought. Piper took extra time with her make-up, adding eye shadow and liner to make them appear luminous and seductive.

Even if this date was the end of her time with Theo, she wanted the fantasy tonight. Theo had been correct in his estimation regarding her life. It was rather lonely. She spent far too many nights by herself. Oh, she had friends and family she adored, and if she wanted company, she could usually find it. Except, at home, she was always alone. She ate her meals, did laundry, swam in her pool, and lived her daily existence, alone. For the most part, she didn't mind it, and even preferred it some days, enjoying her solitude. Yet it didn't mean there were not times—days, and weeks—when she yearned for companionship.

Lately, she'd been considering adopting a dog or a cat to liven up her home life a bit. Except she still traveled quite a bit and didn't think it was fair to need to constantly board a pet or leave them at home with a sitter. Granted, with a dog, she could road trip across the old US of A for her photoshoots, keep herself mainly America-bound. It wasn't like she hadn't already traveled most of the globe anyhow. And her trips abroad were becoming fewer and further in between. So, it was a thought.

Thankfully, she had had the foresight to pack a cocktail dress amidst her camera equipment and outdoorsy type wear that was more suited to camping out in the bush than a five-star dining establishment. Experience had taught her to always be prepared for any scenario when she traveled. The breezy chiffon dress was a simple halter style black number with a crew neckline, which fit her silhouette to perfection and fell to mid-thigh in the front. There was an added, sheer black upper layer that added a bit of flare and then fell below her knees in the back. What she loved most about the dress, though, was the neckline. The golden chain halter circled the base of her collar and gave a nod to the lifestyle.

Then she added the finishing touches to her outfit with a pair of three-inch inky stiletto sandals and dangly gold hoop earrings. She packed a small clutch purse with her phone and her camera —of course, she couldn't go anywhere without it. A professional habit, since she never knew what she might need to photograph. As she left her villa and climbed into her cart, she was beset by huge walloping frogs jumping around in her stomach. This was the first date she'd been on in more than five years. She felt a little bit like a teenager on her first date. Which was ridiculous. She could be the mother of a teenager, and with that thought she was tormented by an old familiar ache. That night so long ago had destroyed not just her sense of self but also the likelihood of her body's ability to conceive children. It wasn't impossible, she had around a three percent chance of conception, but her doctors had explained that the damage to her uterus and female organs had made her body inhospitable for child bearing.

Lately, she had considered adopting or fostering, but had held herself back, like she did with everything else in her life. Which was another one of the reasons why she was considering adopting a dog, figuring it was a place to start, and if that went over well, she could try being responsible for another human.

Theo was a father. After being on the receiving end of his patience and care during her distress that morning, she was in awe of him. He likely was a great dad. He'd ridden out the worst of the storm with her, never faltering or wavering in his steadfast determination to ensure she was all right. Piper knew some of his response was just Theo's inherent good-to-the-bone personality, but she couldn't disregard that some of it was intertwined with the fact he was a parent. The fact that he had a son didn't diminish his appeal. It did quite the opposite. For Piper, it made him an interesting, capable, multi-layered individual who fascinated her. Even a failed marriage in his history didn't lessen the fact that he captivated her. So he'd had a marriage fall apart— she wasn't one to cast stones regarding his past relationships when her own backstory was nothing but a trail of broken hopes and shattered illusions. Let's face it, Piper was the oddball in the relationship quotient, being single, almost forty, and never having taken a trip down the aisle or had a child.

Yet, he'd built a life with another woman, committed himself to her and their future, only to have it end. Had his ex-wife been the one to end the marriage, or had he? What was his ex-wife like? Or his son, for that matter?

Those were some of the million questions swirling in her mind that she wanted to ask him about during their date. She wanted tonight to be a normal date. As much as she feared, deep down, letting Theo into her life and experiencing a relationship with him, even a short-lived one this week, there was a magnetism that drew her to him. It was like she'd had a spell cast on her by a sorceress, and couldn't turn away from him if she tried.

Soon enough, they would return to their normally scheduled lives on different continents at the week's end and she didn't want another regret. She had a lifetime of them built up. And she would regret not knowing him, not experiencing what he had to offer. Even if their date was a farce and an illusion, for tonight, she wanted the fantasy. She desired the pretense of a real relationship with a vengeance that startled even her in its ferocity.

Piper rode the elevator up to the lobby and strolled to the entrance of Master's Pleasure, where she planned to wait for Theo. Near the restaurant's entrance, an obscure artist's beach portrait caught her eye. She studied the painting, off to the right of the hostess's podium. In some respects, the scene reminded her of the great impressionist artists like Monet with the use of color. It was like being in a soft dream. She didn't recognize the signature but snapped a quick photo of the painting. Piper wanted to discover whether this artist had a gallery she could shoot.

Even as entranced as she was by the scene, she felt Theo arrive and his body heat ripple off him as he stood behind her.

"Piper," he murmured near her ear, "I'm glad you came. Let me look at you."

His hand whispered down her arm to clasp her hand as he spun her around. The man packed a wallop in his sharply dressed suit. The smoky gray color accentuated his square jawline that he had yet to shave since he'd been on the island. Not that she minded. She liked his bearded stubble, speckled with hints of gray. She thought it made him seem more sensual, shadowing his lips so that they appeared fuller. And the suit made his broad-shouldered grace appear more debonair.

He brought her hand up to his lips and placed a small kiss on the back. "You look good enough to eat. Shall we? I reserved a table."

She blushed. A few months' shy of forty and he managed to make her blush like a schoolgirl. "Yes, thank you. You do, too."

He flashed a sensual half grin her way and she wanted to fan herself. With a look like that, she almost wanted to forgo dinner and head back to the villa to explore his expression more thoroughly. The hostess led them to a round glossy black table in the center of the restaurant. Piper noted the indiscriminate loops and hidden levers along the lip of the table. They called this place Master's Pleasure for a reason. She ignored the other guests, entranced more by the enigmatic man at her side. His presence obscured everyone else. He held one of the leather chairs out for her, seating her at their table before he took the seat next to her. She was glad he had chosen to sit there instead of across the table.

Looking through the menu, Piper quickly discovered why Theo had sat down where he had. It gave him easier access to… her. He placed a hand on her thigh, teasing the hemline of her dress. The intimate touch made her break out in goosebumps. She didn't mind in the slightest. His touch made her want to curl into him.

She was about to ask him about his day when their waitress, Beth, approached their table. As someone who studied people through camera lenses, Piper felt Beth always appeared just out of focus, like she was wearing a costume that didn't fit her right. She was sweet as one could be, but Piper had also heard through the grapevine that she didn't play with anyone. It made Piper wonder what her story was, because she was sure the camera would love Beth with her midnight hair and startling bright green eyes, complimented by her peaches and cream complexion. Piper was surprised Jared had allowed the beauty to not commit and declare whether she was a submissive or not. Then again, who was she to say, considering she never did a public scene? To each his or her own, she supposed.

"Welcome to Master's Pleasure, Sir. My name is Beth and I will be taking care of you this evening. Would you like to hear today's specials?" Beth asked. It didn't go unnoticed that Beth had not addressed Piper yet but deferred to the Master at the table.

"That would be lovely, proceed," Theo replied, looking every inch the Dom. Piper hid her need to roll her eyes at that. She didn't do tradition very well, and the adherence to formalities and rules she considered asinine tended to make her exasperated.

"Yes, Sir. Today, Chef Davos has prepared crab cakes with a mango chutney and roasted asparagus, fresh caught grouper that's been blackened with a hint of lime, on a bed of sautéed carrots in a white wine demi-glaze and butternut squash risotto. And for dessert, she has whipped up a berry torte with shaved ganache. Can I interest you in a drink to start?" Beth addressed Theo.

Since it was Master's Pleasure, Doms were in complete control of ordering for their submissives. Piper prayed he didn't do something stupid, like order her meal for her. There were some things she considered barbaric practices. It was the twenty-first century and she could order her own damn meal. She submitted her body in the bedroom. Outside of it was another matter entirely. If he turned their date into a 'look at me, I'm Master of the universe' display, it would be a long damn night.

"Let's start with a bottle of the Saddlerock Chardonnay." Then he addressed Piper. "Do you know what you'd like?"

"Yes, I do," she said, relief flooding her veins. She wouldn't be forced into arguing with him and earning herself another spanking. Not that she minded the spankings, she rather enjoyed those, but she didn't know if Theo would discipline her here, in front of everyone, should she buck his command.

He nodded his permission, a dark brow raised in her direction. Like he knew she'd have a conniption fit should he go all lord and master on her. She kept herself from rolling her eyes skyward, but just barely.

"I'd like the sundried tomato chicken with roasted red potatoes and spinach salad," Piper said, handing Beth the menu.

"And for you, Sir?" Beth asked, sliding the menu beneath her right arm as she scribbled the order in her booklet.

"I'd like to try one of the specials tonight. The grouper sounds wonderful."

"Fabulous choice, Sir. I will give your order to the chef, then be back in a flash with your bottle of wine and a basket of Chef Davos' pumpernickel bread," Beth said, taking Theo's menu as well.

"Thank you, little one," Theo said, giving her a gentle smile before turning his attention back to Piper, paying little heed to Beth as she walked away from their table. The warmth in his eyes made Piper's toes curl.

Now that she was his sole focus and there were no longer intruders to their conversation, she asked, "How was your day?"

Theo gave her a contemplative glance before he replied, "It was good. Business as usual when you're a solicitor. I'm managing a few items for Jared and the island. It's really very boring stuff, mountains of paperwork that makes me feel a bit like an old codger by the end of the day. I wasn't kidding about you looking good enough to eat. That's what I plan on doing, right now. I want you to come put that gorgeous ass of yours right here," he patted the table in front of him, "so I can have your succulent pussy as my appetizer."

"What?" This was all wrong and not how this was supposed to go tonight. She shook her head and said, "No, I can't. I told you, I don't do public scenes, ever. I can't have other people around. It makes me have an attack. I'm sorry to disappoint you, but I will never be a sub in that regard." Tears formed in her eyes. Out of the gate, her dream night was already tanking because of the defect in her, as usual.

Theo's hand on her knee had stilled. "So it's because you know that other people are around, or because you see them?"

Piper had never considered that angle. She thought back to her instances and scenes with Peter years ago. Peter had been a very public Dom, always pushing her, enjoying having an audience as he made a sub come undone under his skillful mastery. She'd always been in a room full of people at the club, could see each and every one as they attempted a scene together, then her panic button would go off and she'd melt down. Had he ever tried another way? She'd been in such a state of misery over her what she considered abject failures, she had never questioned Peter's methods, automatically assuming the worst of herself. And her therapist wasn't in the lifestyle, so as good as Caroline was, she had never been able to guide Piper in that area. "Because I could see them, I think."

"What about if you couldn't, see the other guests, I mean? Have you tried that?"

"No," she said, and shook her head.

"Then I have a solution." Theo unfastened his blue tie from his neck, then gestured for her to lean forward. Her heart hammering in her chest, she did as he asked, and glimpsed pride swimming in his cinnamon eyes as he fitted the silk material around her eyes until the room went dark.

Then he guided her until her butt was resting on the lip of the table. "Now, I'm going to help you lie back and then I'm going to eat your pretty pussy. If at any time you feel an attack coming on, use your damn safeword. I want you to focus on me and what I'm doing to you."

She nodded, her heart in her throat as he eased her body back so that she was lying against the table. "I'm not going to restrain you, all right? Just relax, enjoy the pleasure, and let me take care of you."

She wondered why the table was moving beneath her and then realized it wasn't moving at all. She was shaking, trembling in her fear of another possible attack. She'd scaled mountains, taken a boat through the Amazon rainforest, trekked through Incan ruins to get the perfect photograph, and none of it had scared her as much as this did. Part of being submissive was trusting the Dom. After this morning, she owed him her trust. She inhaled a shaky breath as Theo pressed on, speaking softly, "I've got you, love, there's no pain here between us, just pleasure."

Piper nodded and surrendered. Theo's hands toyed with the hem of her dress, grazing her flesh, and delicious twirls of anticipation lit the air around them. Gently, he seduced as his hands trailed along her flesh and he lifted her dress. Cool air caressed her exposed skin as her skirt was bunched up at her waist. Curling his fingertips around the black lace, he drew her panties down her thighs and calves, leaving her sex exposed to everyone in the restaurant.

Piper clenched her fists, battling her anxiety, her heart thumping madly in her chest as she waited for his next move. She could do this. Focus on Theo, not the mind-numbing terror of what might happen.

She sighed and her mouth fell open. Theo's clever hands trailed up her legs with whispered caresses, starting at her calves and then her thighs as he spread them. Her breath clogged in the back of her throat.

"That's it, love. Your body knows what it wants and weeps for my touch," he murmured, then drew his fingers through her folds.

Kinetic pleasure zapped to her core as he teased her flesh, separating her nether lips, stroking under the hood of her clit, and desire flowed in her veins. She gasped when his fingers circled her clitoris, teasing her, but they didn't touch the tiny nub. She squirmed, craving more from him as she surrendered to his sensual torture.

"Mmm, mmm, I'm dining well tonight," Theo mumbled. His baritone voice rumbled deep in her chest, and stoked the flames of her desire. Of their own volition, her hips lifted, yearning for more of his exquisite pleasure. Then a burst of air blew over her clit. She hissed at the sharp bolt of pleasure as it arrowed through her. Theo did it a second, and third time, and she whined at the intensity. Bolts of pleasure made her body throb in agony.

And then his tongue, his wonderful, magic tongue, brushed against her distended nub. Pure, undiluted pleasure blasted through her. She closed her eyes behind the blindfold and gave herself over to Theo's ministrations.

The sounds from the other patrons dimmed. He slurped her clit into his mouth, his teeth grazing the sensitive flesh. His tongue issued a series of fast flicks that left her writhing. Theo laved and teased her flesh with a vigor that stole the very air from her body. Oh god, the man hadn't been joking about making her part of his meal.

The impromptu blindfold was a godsend. The restaurant attendees receded until her entire world revolved around him. It allowed her to concentrate on just Theo and what his gifted tongue was doing to her pussy.

He lapped at her sex, savoring her intimate flesh with relish. She wanted more, canting her hips, thrusting against the torrid ministrations and the deliciously wicked cunnilingus he was performing. Piper canted her hips, trying to feed him more of her pussy as he licked her labia and clit. Pleasure multiplied with each stroke of his tongue. Then he penetrated her sheath, thrusting his tongue deep inside her channel. Her mouth opened on a moan and stayed that way. He fervently thrust, fucking her pussy with his tongue. She couldn't have stopped her mewls if she'd tried. The man was a god among mortals when it came to performing oral.

He nibbled, licked, and thrust, driving her body higher and higher. Theo feasted on her flesh like she was a fine delicacy and he was a starving man. Over and over she moaned, her heels digging into his back as she rolled her hips. When his fingers joined the fray, thrusting, and plunging into her clasping channel as he rapidly tongued her swollen clit, Piper wailed.

Theo thrust his fingers and bit down on her abused nub. A shower of sparks erupted as she came.

"Sir, oh god!" she cried, her body vibrating and rocking as waves of ecstasy barreled through her. The tidal wave swamped her, infusing her body with bursts of pleasure as she shook.

Theo didn't stop until the last ripple of her body clenched around his thrusting fingers. It was only then that he withdrew his mouth and fingers, then slid her dress back into place. She limply lay against the table, stunned, while claps and hoots from the other guests erupted around them.

Piper couldn't believe it. She'd performed a scene in public. Maybe she wasn't as broken as she'd believed. A smiled bloomed on her face as Theo helped her sit up and removed her blindfold. His hand cupped her chin and he tenderly brushed his lips against hers, her flavor coating his lips. There was something so intimate and stirring about tasting herself on his lips.

"You did well," he said, pride swimming in his cinnamon depths.

"What, no 'I told you so's?" she asked as he helped her off the table and back into her chair. Beth approached the table and wiped the ebony surface down with a wet cloth, which carried the distinct tang of bleach. Once the table was clean, Beth delivered their wine, placing a wine bucket and two glasses on the table. She uncorked the bottle and poured a glass for each of them, handing one to Theo first for approval. The aroma from the freshly baked, warm bread wafted over Piper and made her stomach growl as a steaming basket was placed on the table followed by small appetizer plates, silverware, and fresh butter.

Theo served her a piece of bread first before serving himself and said, "No. Because that would imply that I didn't believe you could do it, and I did. It's a step, but one in the right direction."

Piper digested his words, applying butter on her warm slice of bread, and replied, "It doesn't mean I'm ready to do a full scene in the club, though."

"I understand that. Tonight, we pushed your boundaries and you met them head on like a champ, which is a good thing. Perhaps you need a few more small, mini-scenes like this one to help you overcome your fears and waylay any chance of a panic attack happening. Then again, maybe not—there's always a chance that this method won't work in a vibrant club setting, but I think it's worth a try. Don't you?"

For the first time in an inordinately long time, Piper felt hope, hope for a future that might no longer stretch out before her as an unending sea of loneliness. Maybe, just maybe, she could have a relationship with a Dom, perform scenes in clubs, and not freak out. Maybe she could submit more of herself and perhaps even find a Dom who would want to keep her. Maybe she might even find one who would love her and would want a life with her. Did she think risking a potential attack was worth it? Unequivocally, yes. "I do. I won't lie though, it scares me. As you witnessed this morning, when I have an attack, my therapist has said it's like what soldiers experience with a PTSD episode, where I'm not even present but reliving the horror of that night."

Theo studied her, absorbing her words as Beth delivered their meal. "Well, that's why we do this in baby steps. I will be with you every step of the way. Remember, Rome wasn't built in a day, and from what you've indicated, the attack was severe. Give yourself permission to take your recovery slowly, to work on it in stages. Why does it have to be a race to the finish line? Who are you trying to outrun, yourself? That night? What if, by attempting to blast through it as fast as possible, you've missed a crucial step that would help eradicate a subtle cause behind the attacks entirely? You'll never know unless you try. In fact, I think we should repeat this exercise, here at the restaurant in the morning, and perhaps again tomorrow evening. We can do it as often as needed until you're comfortable with it, and then we can take it to the next level and progress. I will help you as much as I can while I'm here on the island, and we'll take it slow."

"Sounds like a good plan. How did you get so wise?" she said, joy spreading in her being. He truly wanted to help her—not to add a notch in his belt like a conquering hero, but for her benefit.

Theo studied her as he took a bite of his dinner and then said, "I think it comes with being a parent and watching your child struggle. Jacob's fine, but there was a time in primary school where he wanted to be as fast as everyone else on the football field—or soccer, as you Americans call it—and had to learn to pace himself. He went through a significant amount of trial and error before he figured out how to make himself better."

She could see how much he loved his son. It was right out in the open as he contemplated his wine glass before lifting it to his lips. Piper would bet it had been Theo out on the field with his son, day after day, helping Jacob overcome a perceived deficiency and become a better player. Theo wasn't at all like she'd initially assumed him to be. He was so much more. And she wanted to know him, whatever part of himself he was willing to share with her.

"Tell me about him. Your son. What's he like? How old is he? Why did you and his mom get divorced?" she asked, getting a bit flustered at the last bit. She was surprised by the pang of jealousy she felt toward his ex-wife.

"Diane and I met while I was in law school. We fell for each other rather quickly. I did love her and she me, although even at the beginning of our relationship, deep down I knew I needed more physically, that I had what I thought were eccentric tastes. I hadn't embraced my dominant nature at that point, and didn't even know what to call it then. I was what you might call an uptight Englishman," he teased her.

She laughed and lifted her wineglass, toasting him. "You said it, not me, Sir."

He chuckled and continued, "Right you are. Anyway, I repressed my nature because I thought I had to. We were happy, and married when I was twenty-eight. Jacob came along a year later. He's a lot like his mum."

"I'm sure there's some of you in him, too."

Theo nodded, then twined his hand with hers, stroking his thumb over her wrist, showing her how pleased he was by her words and said, "There is, but anyway… I was working at my first firm as a junior solicitor when a case came across my desk. It was a simple estate planning type of will, very boring stuff, but the client requested that I meet with him at his estate. And that was when I was introduced to the lifestyle. The older gent was a Master wanting to ensure his slave was cared for in the event of his demise. He'd just learned that he had Parkinson's disease and knew it would lead to his eventual death. As he showed me around the estate, his private dungeon was part of the tour. Seeing his dungeon ignited what I'd tried to suppress for too many years to count. After that, I met with my client on a few more occasions, begging him for instruction, which he so kindly gave. He was the one who introduced me to Declan and Jared. Seems like a lifetime ago. From there, I learned everything I could about the lifestyle. Then, one night, I brought what I had learned to my marriage bed. I needed it so much I couldn't see anything else, and I wanted Diane to be a part of this whole new world that had finally opened up for me."

His fingers clenched hers as he stopped.

"But?" Piper prodded him, needing to hear the rest of his story.

"Diane is a lovely woman, steadfast, true, but she's about as vanilla as one could be when it comes to bedroom activities. When I broached the subject of trying to include some of the things I had learned, she flatly refused. Now, admittedly, I felt like a sod for even broaching the topic. But after that night, our marriage soured. Mainly it was my fault because I became resentful that she denied me what I needed. In the end, the lure of my needs was too potent. I think it was because they'd been suppressed for so long. It doesn't excuse my actions in any way, but after that I began to seek what I needed physically from a woman outside of my marriage. I felt like a heel, going to clubs and getting my rocks off with submissives who weren't my wife, but I also felt whole for the first time in my life. It was intoxicating to finally embrace my dominant nature. As I did so, my marriage crumbled around me.

"Eventually, it was Diane who asked me for a divorce. She allowed me to share full custody of our son with the stipulation that I don't display my sexual preferences in his vicinity until he is eighteen. So, the bulk of my interactions with submissives has been at clubs, parties and the like over the last decade."

Piper was appalled for Theo. How could his ex-wife make him agree to a stipulation like that? She said, "I can't believe she would ask you that. I'm not saying a child needs to—or in fact wants to—know how their parents get their rocks off, but she's made you hide who you are all this time?"

Theo shrugged and said, "It's not so bad. I do have a dungeon in my home, an old wine cellar I converted that my son knows nothing about. He doesn't know the room even exists. I made sure it was a hidden room. But due to the stipulation, I've been careful and rather circumspect in who I will even bring into my home. It's not worth losing my boy over."

The fact that he would put his son above his own happiness and satisfaction astonished Piper. Theo was a deep in the bones good man. Upon first meeting him she had believed he was just a stuffy Brit with Alpha Dom tendencies. But he wasn't stuffy at all. He played his cards close to his chest but then again, so did she. Theo reminded her of a blue flame. His fires burned hotter and deeper than most flames. And she didn't care about his infidelity. It was obvious that he had unintentionally been atoning for his actions by agreeing to his ex-wife's stipulation and then following it to the letter.

"How old is he now?" she asked, picturing a boy who was Theo's spitting image.

"Fifteen, going on twenty-five. It's goes so much faster than you might think. One day, their chubby little hands are wrapped around your fingers as they are trying to walk for the first time, and the next they are attending secondary school, captain of the rugby team, and looking at potential universities."

"Do you see him often?"

Theo nodded and said, "As often as I can. My home is near him and his mum. He tends to stay with me on the weekends, even the ones that aren't part of the divorce decree. That's one thing Diane has never denied me, or fought me over: access to our son."

It explained so much about Theo. What with the stipulation, and his son living in his home on the weekends, when most clubs were in full swing, it was no wonder he wasn't in a committed relationship. Piper had been right, he was a bit of an island. She said, "It's nice that you're so close to him. That you've stayed in his life."

Theo shrugged and replied, "He's my son. Just because his mum and I didn't work out, doesn't mean I wanted him to grow up without me around. Jacob is the best part of my life. Work and all the rest are just fillers."

"And you mentioned that Diane had remarried. What's her husband like?" Piper hated that she was so curious about his ex-wife. It was obvious that whatever relationship they had together was over and they'd both moved on.

"Donald's a fine bloke. He's been good for Diane and for Jacob, too."

"But?"

"There's a pain that comes with watching another man help raise your child. Donald's not an ogre and has been good for Jacob, but seeing your son admire and look up to another father figure—I'm not going to lie, it's had its moments. But all in all, I think it is making my son a better young man. He has two examples of what it means to be a man, even if I'm a bit dodgy at times," Theo joked with a half-grin.

It had hurt him far more than he was letting on. Piper wanted to wrap her arms around him and comfort his hurts, but because of their audience, she squeezed his hand gently instead, and said, "I think he's lucky to have you. Not all fathers want to stay in their child's life after a divorce. Mine didn't. It's not that he didn't love us, my siblings and me, he just moved on."

"How many siblings do you have?" Theo asked, taking a swallow of his wine and finishing his glass.

"Two younger sisters. We're all California girls, at least at heart. JoAnn moved with her husband, Todd, to New Mexico a while back for his job. And then the baby of our family, Christina, lives in San Diego with her husband, Julian."

"Are you close?"

"Yes, we are. Mom lives near Christina, but our Dad died three years ago."

"Sorry, I know how that is. Both my parents are gone, Mum just two years ago, and they never gave me any brothers or sisters. I think they tried but Mum had a hard time with my delivery and it messed her body up a bit. They were wonderful, devoted to each other, and to me. She would have liked you, I think," Theo said, pushing his empty plate back.

Warmth suffused Piper at his words. "I'm sure, given how well she did with you, that she was an incredible woman."

"That she was."

Beth intervened then and asked, "Can I get you any dessert this evening, Sir?"

"Piper?" Theo asked, still holding her hand in his.

"No, thank you. I'm stuffed." And there was still food left over on her plate. She'd rather make Theo her dessert, but she wasn't going to say that in front of Beth.

Theo glanced at Beth with a congenial smile and said, "I

think that will be it for the evening. If you could charge the bill to my lodgings, please?"

"Certainly, Sir. Let me get the bill for you to sign-off on." Beth left and headed to one of the registers behind the bar area.

"Thank you, Sir. Dinner was lovely." The night had exceeded Piper's expectations. It was one she'd remember and cherish long after their time together had come to a close. The thought of not seeing him after this week made her chest ache. Before Piper could say anything more, Beth returned to their table with the check and handed it to Theo. He flipped the black leather book open and signed the bill before passing it back to Beth.

And then he gave Piper a hungry, sensual glance and asked, "Ready?"

For him, she was beyond ready for anything he might have in mind. She wanted to thank him, show her appreciation for the night. And not because she felt she owed him, but because she wanted him, wanted to submit to his dark desires all night long.

"Yes," she murmured, accepting his hand as he helped her from the chair. He led her out of the restaurant, placing his hand against her lower back, and just that simple touch ignited a slow burn in her blood. They rode the elevator down in companionable silence and then exited the hotel when the doors slid open on the ground level.

Theo steered her toward the bank of golf carts.

"I will follow behind you in my cart to your place," he said after depositing her inside hers.

"That would be nice," she said, her blood pressure spiking at the promise of the upcoming decadence. She started the cart with a sigh, and drove with Theo tailing her, his headlights flashing in her rear-view mirror.

He'd shifted her paradigm tonight. Piper grappled with what it meant for her and her life. Did it mean that she could be more of a 'normal' submissive? Could she start engaging more at Dungeon Pleasures in Pasadena? Or was her ability to do a scene related to Theo? Was it his touch that had engendered her transformation tonight? It had been one mini-scene. She shouldn't allow herself to get excited over just one small victory and get ahead of herself. Just that morning, she'd had a full-blown episode. The first in almost a year. Maybe if she performed ten or twenty or more complete scenes with no regressions, then perhaps she could break out the champagne and consider taking it one step further.

But she couldn't downplay the importance of tonight, either. It all revolved around Theo and how he made her feel. Safe. Even with her episode that morning. She'd already been fighting her anxiety before he'd made it onto the beach. And yes, it had happened because she'd allowed herself to feel for him and surrendered herself completely last night. It was not his fault, but hers—and her own messed up psyche.

Yet she'd enjoyed every minute of her submission.

Theo had brought her back from the brink of madness and terror. There were few people in her life who even knew about her episodes, and most didn't have any knowledge or experience of how to bring her out of one. Yet Theo had battered against her terror until he reached her, pulling her to safety and holding her until the storm of her past abated.

He may be a bit of a stuffy Brit but he was also dedicated, sturdy, and an altogether decent man. The fact that he had kept his lifestyle apart from his home life for his son. That amazed Piper. She didn't expect generosity of spirit and self-sacrifice from a Master, especially one who was such a traditionalist and stickler for rules. And as someone who had made it her life's work to capture a person's character through her telephoto lenses, she was aware that honorable, kind men like him didn't come along every day.

The man was layers deep, with a keen mind and a wholly sensual nature that he had no trouble unleashing around her. Would he want more tonight? Could she convince him to join her in her villa? She parked the cart and disembarked, waiting for him near the elevator to do the same. Shivers raced along her spine. Did he have more planned, or was he just dropping her at her place like on a traditional, vanilla date?

In the shadowed light, Theo appeared downright wicked as he approached her. His desire was clear and written all over his face. He had no intention of leaving her alone tonight.

Chapter 8

Theo invaded her space. With his large body, he backed her into the elevator and slapped the interior button to ascend but never stopped moving and pressed her up against the wall. Her body purred as he claimed her lips.

His sinful mouth ravaged hers as the elevator took them up to her place. She leaned in to him, hungry for more of his touch. The man kissed her with his entire being, ensuring she felt every tendril and spark of kinetic energy as it flowed between them. Need erupted inside her as she returned his passionate kiss. Piper exulted in being able to touch him, in the fact that her hands weren't restrained so she could feel his power and potency. Her hands worked at the buttons on his dress shirt, yearning to feel his chest, his body, all of him beneath her touch. She wanted to commit him to memory, to remember when she was home in Santa Barbara, alone and needing sustenance.

He growled into her mouth as she teased the flat disks of his nipples, scratching her nails through his pelt of dark hair. Theo hoisted her up and she wrapped her legs around his waist as he carried her from the elevator. He made a direct beeline for her bed, stripping her dress off over her head as he transported them with his determined stride.

Hurry, hurry, hurry.

The words played in her mind like a mantra. Piper was beyond ready, needing to feel him. She shoved at his dress coat and shirt, nearly ripping them from him in her impatience.

He chuckled roguishly at her eagerness as he released her mouth. She whined in protest. Then he tugged her nipple into his mouth as he lay her down on the bed. She arched her back, feeding him her mound of flesh. Her fingers slid into his feather-soft dark hair, holding his lips at her breast. Christ, the man had a talented mouth. Desire raced through her veins.

Theo released her breast. He hovered over her, the sensual hunger in his expression causing every nerve ending in her body to tremble in anticipation. But it had become more than just scratching an itch for Piper. Theo moved her, not just with his touch, but with who he was at the core of his being. Her hand caressed his cheek, marveling over the strength in his jawline, marveling at him, and knowing deep inside that there was no place else she'd rather be. He gripped her hand, placing a tender kiss in her palm and rubbing his stubble-lined jaw against it.

Then Theo acted like an explorer, caressing, tasting, and nibbling on every part of her body. He suckled her neglected breast until that nipple pointed proudly toward the ceiling from his attention. He nibbled on the delicate undersides of her breasts, teasing her with his tongue. Placing playful love bites over her abdomen, Theo monitored her every reaction to his touch.

By the time his dark head was hovering between her splayed thighs, Piper's blood was humming in eagerness. Her arousal and awareness of Theo were tantamount. The world outside her bedroom could be sinking into the ocean, with the world under attack by space aliens, and she wouldn't know it. In the confines of her bedroom, they built a new world where it was only the two of them and the pleasure they sought together. Theo teased her inner thighs, playfully tickling her flesh and she squealed, "Theo, Sir."

He chuckled, giving her a rakish, wicked glance full of sensual intent. Then his mouth descended.

"Oh god," she cried, and her head fell back against the sheets as his mouth latched on to her clitoris with such ferocity, her body coiled and spun into intoxicating pleasure that revved her body into a near trance-like, euphoric state where only pleasure existed. Her legs fell open further, granting him an all-access pass. She thrust her hips as her need spiraled higher. He found that one spot as he stroked her that drove her over the edge of reason.

"Theo, Sir, oh god," she moaned, writhing beneath his deft touch. She grabbed at the sheets as he held her hips steady, not letting her escape his carnal caress. Piper strained, her body drawn taut as her passion escalated into mindless territory. Her entire being was Theo's to command, and it didn't bother her. Not. One. Bit.

"Ah, Sir!" She arched her back as ecstasy blasted her system and her body shook with the force of her climax. But Theo didn't stop eating her as he made her pussy his banquet. He had discovered a new way to torture her, by relentlessly giving her mind-blowing oral sex and not stopping.

Piper climaxed beneath his mouth again and again. Her clit became so swollen from his arduous attentions, the tiny bud ached. It had to stop—she needed his cock, needed to feel him inside her. Her body rent asunder with her latest climax, she finally caved.

She begged and nearly wept, "Please, Sir, please fuck me. I can't take any more. Please."

Theo lifted his head from between her thighs, his chin coated with her cream. "Took you long enough, love—not that I mind, as I could eat your sweet cunt all night long."

Then it dawned on her. This had been another lesson. He'd been waiting for her to ask him for what she wanted. She shook her head at her own stubbornness. Theo rose and knelt back on his haunches, his erection jutting and waving at her. She licked her lips, yearning to taste the drop of cum leaking from his crest.

"Another time, Piper, I will let you suck my dick all you want. I need to feel your pussy too badly right now. On your hands and knees, I want to watch that gorgeous ass of yours as I fuck you," he commanded, his accent thick with his desire.

Piper needed no urging. She rolled onto her hands and knees, presenting him with her backside, lifting her rear up. Theo grasped the two halves of her ass, massaging the globes, tracing the outline of her tattoo, and teasing her with his dick. He rubbed his length through her labia, parting the lips of her sex. She whined at the feel of his crown sliding through her swollen folds, and dug her hands into the mattress.

"Sir, please. Please fuck me," she begged, beyond reason or shame. Her body was engulfed in a passion so potent, all she could think about was feeling him pound away inside her. She canted her hips, needing more friction, more everything from him.

"Since you asked so nicely, how could I refuse?" The smooth head of his shaft pressed against her entry. She moaned as Theo's hands held her steady as he penetrated her. She groaned. He felt so damn good. The way his cock filled her, encountering no resistance as he thrust forward until his balls pressed against her engorged clit.

Then, while he was fully embedded in her pussy, his right hand smacked her butt cheek. Her walls clenched around his shaft and pleasure ricocheted through her. He did it again, and she keened. And again. Piper grunted, her body engulfed in pleasure-pain so acute, it was as though she existed in another world. At the next thwack of his hand, Piper's body imploded.

"Sir, oh god," she wailed, her body trembling, her pussy

clasping at his cock. And only then did he start shuttling his length in and out of her channel. He held her hips steady as he set a bruising rhythm. Piper dug her fingers deeper into the mattress, holding on as he hammered his shaft. She knew she'd have bruises on her hips from where his fingers dug in, holding her body in place. But she didn't care. She reveled in his unrestrained passion as he brutally pumped his hips, pounding his flesh inside her. The bed shook from his hard thrusts. Or maybe that was her—she didn't care, as long as he didn't stop.

Piper's body spiraled higher and higher. She knew she could only hold on a little longer. "Sir, please," she whined.

His large hands moved and gripped her shoulders, the new angle making her eyes roll back in her head. He grunted as his tempo increased and he jack hammered his cock inside her quivering depths. Harder, faster, he rammed his shaft, his crown striking the lip of her womb. Theo's cock swelled in her channel as he pistoned his hips and he growled, "Come for me."

He slammed home. Piper keened as stars exploded in her body.

"Sir!" she screamed as her body exploded in blistering waves of ecstasy so pronounced and deep, Piper was certain the dead could hear her cries.

"Ah," Theo bellowed. His body jerked and strained. Hot liquid spurted inside her quaking tissues, setting off another round of pleasure bursts. He thrust as he came, his cock juddering and jolting inside her. Then he leaned forward until his chest was flush against her back, pulling her body close, keeping his softening length buried in her channel as he pulled her down onto her side.

Theo gently turned her head and claimed her lips in an affectionate kiss, pouring himself into the embrace. When he released her mouth, his heavy-lidded, satisfied gaze studied her, his knuckles softly caressing her cheek. That organ Piper had long denied stood on the ledge… and jumped over the side. As much as she feared it, she couldn't deny how much she wanted this man. Her eyes grew heavy from her over indulgence in Theo.

"Sleep, love. I'll be here in the morning," he said, kissing her forehead, and settling himself behind her. But he didn't let her go, holding her within his embrace as she drifted off to sleep.

A girl could certainly get used to a life like this.

Chapter 9

Always an early riser, Piper yawned and stretched, her muscles gloriously achy after last night. She lay flat on her stomach and heard Theo's deep, even breathing beside her. She shifted her head, pushing her hair away from her face.

He took her breath away. The lines around his eyes and mouth were softened in sleep, making him look younger. His hair was rumpled and she yearned to run her hands through it. He lay supine on his back, one arm tossed over his head, the other beside his waist. Even asleep, the power and potency of his form didn't diminish. If anything, it was even more startling in its resiliency as he rested. She had to capture it, him, before she did something stupid like blubber all over him and cuddle him. Piper had to remind herself that the relationship was a mirage. A beautiful, intoxicating one, but a façade that wouldn't last past this week, even as she secretly wished for more everything with him.

Piper grabbed her digital camera from the nightstand. She knelt over him, snapping his image. She'd call the photographs 'A Dom at Rest' or something of that nature once she'd developed them. At least, that was what she told herself as the camera clicked in her hands. In reality, she wanted to remember this moment, remember him and the way he made her feel after such a long drought of just existing. Piper moved quietly around him, snapping images from different angles. There was one shot she wanted, but was worried about how he would take it. She chewed on her bottom lip for all of two seconds.

Screw it.

Piper straddled his waist, getting the direct overhead shots that she wanted. But then, as she clicked away, a large hand slid onto her thigh and she felt his shaft harden, lengthen beneath her form. Piper didn't let go of the camera as he cracked open his eyes, his mouth sliding into a carnal smile. Her breath caught as she captured the unbridled lust on his face.

"Morning, love. Why don't you put that thing down and greet me properly?" he said, rubbing his hips and his now impressive erection against her pelvis.

She bit her lip, not stopping her picture taking. "Give me a moment, Sir. I'd like to photograph you while I do."

"As long as I get to capture you, too, have at it," Theo murmured, his voice cloudy with lust.

Piper held her camera with one hand, then lifted her hips, reached down with her free hand, clasped his shaft, and fit his crown at her pussy. His hands braced her hips, holding her steady, and helped her seat herself on his erection. She hissed as she thrust, his cock furrowing inside her. Once she was seated, she took a deep breath and then canted her hips slowly. This was not the brutal fucking from the night before. It was languorous, so that she felt every blessed inch as her pelvis tilted and accepted him.

And through it all, she snapped pictures of Theo, capturing the look on his face when he was buried so deep inside her it was as if he had become part of her body. His concentration, as he flexed and undulated beneath her, giving her such potent intensity behind his slow thrusts. Piper felt every remaining barrier she had been holding in place to protect herself shatter. She flexed her Kegel muscles, squeezing his member, and he groaned. She did it a second and then a third time, capturing the look of bliss and hunger on his face.

"My turn," Theo growled, and took the camera from her. She didn't fight him on it. She needed more friction, more movement as her desire for him rose.

Piper now had the front of the camera to contend with, which was an unusual feeling. She understood all too well how much the camera lens could capture, but she chose to ignore the shutter clicks. Instead, she focused on his lips, his body, the mind-melting feel of his cock plunging inside her sheath.

"That's it, love, ride me," Theo commanded.

She did as he ordered, undulating her hips, thrusting in a sensual rhythm, and putting her hands on his chest as she increased her pace. She lunged and rolled her pelvis, surrendering to the urgency building inside her. He felt so good, so right. Her eyes slid closed as a swath of pleasure electrified her body.

"Gorgeous, now kiss me," Theo ordered on a groan, still snapping photos of her writhing above him.

At his command, she leaned forward until her mouth was hovering an inch from his. Theo held her camera out to the side. Then he reached up with his free hand, grasped the back of her head, and brought her mouth down upon his. He claimed her lips, plundering her mouth, thrusting his tongue inside her dark recesses, and he captured it all on film.

Then he released her mouth and said, "That's enough with this thing. I want to fuck you properly and I need my hands to do it."

She removed the camera from his grip, hit a few buttons, and then set it on the nightstand. As soon as it left her hands, Theo pulled her back down until her face was suspended above his. He gripped the back of her head, his eyes boring into hers as he thrust and rolled his hips, pistoning his cock in hammered strokes, striking the lip of her cervix in an almost painful fashion. But the pain contorted into intense pleasure. Her mouth opened on a shuddered gasp. Her nails dug into his chest as she rode him. But he held her close so that they were eye to eye. And then he crushed her mouth to his, surrounding her with his essence as the storm of their lovemaking accelerated to maddening heights. She writhed at the frantic, wild pace.

Theo's cock slammed within her depths, the crest almost touching her womb. She keened into his mouth. "Mmm."

Then Theo rolled her body so she was on her back, and withdrew his cock.

"Sir?" she whimpered, so near climax she wanted to sob with frustration.

"Give me a sec." He yanked open the nightstand drawer and smiled. "I'm going to fuck your little rosebud. My cock has ached to feel your snug rosette squeezing me."

He withdrew a tube of lubricant and shifted, pulling pillows down from near the headboard.

"Lift your hips, that's a girl," he said as he shoved them under her butt. The pillows tilted her hips up above thirty degrees, which would give him deeper access to her anus.

Once he had her hips in position, slanted at the angle he desired, he slicked lube around her rosette, then pressed his fingers forward. She bit her lower lip at the slice of discomfort. It had been ages since she'd had anal, but she wanted to with him. She wanted it all with Theo. She breathed deep, allowing her body to relax as he stretched her back hole with first one finger, then two, before finally adding a third digit. He stretched her, working his fingers in and out. Her mouth fell open on a moan as pleasure underscored any discomfort and her body accommodated him.

"That's it. You're so tight, I can't wait to feel you around my cock." Then he removed his fingers and placed his crown at her tiny rosebud. He slicked more lube over his shaft. And then he pressed forward, canting his pelvis, and pushing past the resistant tissues in her anus. He worked his cock inside, withdrawing and thrusting, his teeth gritted until he was embedded in her rear.

"Christ, you feel like silk hugging my dick, love," Theo growled, sweat slicking his chest.

Then he withdrew and thrust, her nerve endings exploding in sweet, fiery agony that zinged a direct line to her pussy. Her core throbbed as he shuttled his member in and out of her back channel. Her body was engulfed in a sea of passion, her hips rising to meet his thrusts as he pounded in her rear. She wanted—needed—her release in the worst way. She mewled and moaned, riding the waves of pleasure only he seemed able to give her. From his kneeling position, with one of her legs tossed over his shoulder for a better angle, he shocked her whole system when he slipped three fingers inside her pussy while his cock burrowed deep inside her ass.

"Oh god," she screamed, her head falling back on the bed as her hips arched up to meet his dual penetration. He screwed her in tandem, thrusting inside her pussy as his cock withdrew, and then he slamming his cock home as his fingers retreated. Over and over, until she was so full of him that her mind vacated the premises as she surrendered to all the pleasure he could provide.

Theo's tempo increased as his ardor rose alongside hers, his movements becoming less controlled as his lust overrode everything.

"Come for me," he commanded and pinched her clit as he sank inside her ass with brutal, unyielding force.

The slice of pleasure-pain started a chain reaction, detonating bombs inside her body. Her pussy compressed around his thrusting fingers, her ass clenched around his plunging cock, and —*oh, my, god.*

"Oh, Sir!" She arched her back, her body quaking. Her climax shook her foundation to its core. Over and over, explosions rocked her system.

"Piper," Theo roared, straining above her as his cock elongated and spewed jets of hot cum into her grasping ass. He poured inside her, thrusting, filling her back channel.

She entered a hazy plain of sublime satisfaction as he slumped over her, his breathing heavy while his heart rate returned to normal. Piper purred against his neck as he gathered her close. The last forty-eight or so hours had been damn near the best of her life, and she didn't want this euphoric state to ever end. She burrowed against his chest, content and happy, cuddling in his arms.

Theo murmured, his voice thick with satisfaction, "That was without a doubt the best morning wake-up I've had in a while. Thank you. Join me in the shower, eh, and I promise to wash every nook and cranny."

Her stomach chose that moment to growl and he chuckled. "And then I promise to feed you at Master's Pleasure."

She stiffened at the thought of leaving their cozy cocoon of paradise. It wasn't just that he would have her do a small scene again, it was also that she simply wanted to stay here, where it was only the two of them.

He shifted until he could study her face and asked, "What's wrong?"

"I'd rather just stay in bed all day with you," she admitted, wishing that she could convince him and not break the spell of their fabulous night together.

His eyes heated. "As much as I wish we could do precisely that, I have work with Jared that I must see to today. Otherwise," he leaned in close and nipped at her bottom lip, "you wouldn't even have to ask—because I wouldn't be letting you leave."

Her eyes closed and she sighed. He was right. Damnit. She had a job to complete as well. Duty first. But still, she wanted a full day with him. No work, just play. It was the whole 'if wishes were beggars' thing.

"Then let's take that shower," she conceded. She didn't have to tell him twice as he carted her into the bathroom.

He held true to his promise—he kept doing that—and did indeed wash every nook and cranny of hers, more than once. Then he left her place to dress for his day, only to return looking rather dapper in his black trousers and dress shirt. She'd munched on an apple as she dressed, too hungry to wait for breakfast. Besides, she'd eat there as well, what with all the calories she was burning, she needed the energy or she'd wilt. And she wanted everything to be perfect so she could catalog it in her memory banks.

Theo helped her load her equipment in the cart and drove them to breakfast at Master's Pleasure. When he was going to leave her camera bags in the cart, she shook her head.

"They should be fine there," he said.

"No, sorry, but they need to come with me. That's twenty thousand dollars' worth of equipment and I'll not chance leaving it out here," she explained, hefting her bags from the cart.

"At least let me, Piper," he said, holding his hands out and not budging until she conceded and held out the handles to him.

"See, that wasn't so difficult," he murmured, giving her a small smile. It was, actually, more than he realized, but Piper didn't want to upset the delicate balance between them.

In the restaurant, after they ordered breakfast, Theo ate her pussy until she came, screaming his name. The restaurant wasn't nearly as busy this morning as it had been the previous evening, but he used his tie again as a blindfold. Piper still felt it was a victory that she didn't clam up or have an episode and was able to give herself over into his capable hands.

Breakfast arrived shortly after her climax. Unlike dinner the night before, this meal was more hurried, with Theo checking his watch for the time so they didn't dawdle.

"Sorry, Jared has a spate of meetings, otherwise we could take our time," he explained as he signed for the bill again.

"It's no problem. We'll have plenty of time tonight," she murmured, standing with him. He shot her a heated glance and then escorted her from the restaurant. He ushered her into the elevator and kissed her soundly. When the doors dinged as they opened on the ground level, he released her lips, regret filling his eyes.

"Meet me at the restaurant for dinner at six, please. Feel free to use my cart today," he said, his gaze warm even as he withdrew from their embrace. Was it wrong of her that she wanted to tell Jared and his photos to go to hell and convince Theo to play hooky? Probably.

Instead of trying to entice him to be very bad today, she bowed her head with a slight tilt and acknowledgement that she considered him her Dom. Then she said, "Thank you. I will."

Theo kissed her brow, pressed the button for the top floor, and saluted her as the doors closed. Piper inhaled a steadying breath. She kept having to remind herself that he wasn't hers to keep. But Christ almighty, the man made it difficult. With every fiber of her being, she wanted to keep him, wanted to belong to him and him to her.

She reluctantly climbed into the cart and headed off for the day, where she used her work as a distraction to keep her mind off Theo. It didn't work much, as she found herself smiling more in that single day than she likely had all year.

OVER THE NEXT THREE DAYS, Piper and Theo established a routine. Every morning, after what was without a doubt the best sex of her life, they would head to the island restaurant for breakfast. As they waited for their meal, Theo would do a small scene with her at the table, from eating her pussy to a full on power bang from behind. Then, after breakfast, Theo would escort her to the cart, carrying her camera equipment for her, kiss her, and then head to Jared's office. At night, they reconvened at the restaurant for dinner where, once again, Theo would perform a mini-scene with her while they waited for their meal.

Then they drove back to her villa, where a remarkable number of his items, like an extra toothbrush in her bathroom, had made their way into her place. She didn't mind but enjoyed the coziness of it. She laughed more, found she was enjoying life more over those three days than she had in twenty years. It was like she was imbibing all life had to offer her during her time with Theo. She felt an urgency to soak up as much of his lovemaking as possible. He tested her boundaries, and even broke out a cane one night. They were so in sync, she wondered how she had ever gone without him. Piper knew all too well what her life had been like before he had entered it. And it worried her how attached she'd become to him.

They only had three days left before he had to go back to England. Neither of them had broached the topic of their week almost being up. But they were both feeling it, as her tender backside could attest to today. She'd snapped at him after dinner last night, where one thing had led to another and he'd tanned her backside before he screwed her brains out.

Theo woke her with a kiss on her forehead. She was already awake, knowing precisely when he'd left her bed.

"Get some rest. Jared asked me to join him for a breakfast meeting today. Meet me at the restaurant tonight. I'd like to discuss some things," Theo said, his gaze unreadable for the first time in days.

Her heart trembled at the disturbance to their routine. "All right, I will be there."

"That's a love," he murmured. He tenderly stroked her cheek before he retreated and left her place.

Fear churned in her belly. Did he plan to end things already? Make a clean break now? What did he want to discuss? And how had her world become so enmeshed with his, and she so dependent upon him?

Chapter 10

Duty called as Theo drove his cart to the main hotel and then rode the lift to the top floor. He was joining Jared and Naomi in their penthouse for a private breakfast. He stopped on his way and retrieved the file with Jared's Last Will and Testament, along with a few other documents Jared had asked him to draw up for the pending engagement.

Seriously, the Doms of the DFC were dropping like flies, all getting hitched.

He knocked on the door. It was Naomi who answered, barefoot, her clothing a bit disheveled and her lips swollen.

"Good morning, Sir, won't you please come in?" Naomi said, blushing, her dark curls swaying as they framed her exotic face. She was a beauty. Theo could see what Jared saw in her.

"Thank you, Naomi. Something smells lovely," he said as he entered. The small foyer opened up into a wide living room done in rich dark browns and reminded him of England. Since he and Piper had begun having their nightly marathon sessions, he'd been eating like a freaking horse and the smells emanating from the kitchen had him salivating. He'd already had an apple on the way in just to take the edge off his hunger.

He liked the understated wealth of the penthouse, but he also noticed a collection of wildflowers in a Waterford vase on the coffee table, and a bright red chenille blanket draped over the leather chaise near the large bay of windows. Likely Naomi's doing. Women had a way of turning a functional space into a comfortable home.

Jared strutted into the living room, appearing far too pleased with himself and deep in the bone happy. Had Theo ever been that blissed out? Then it struck him between the eyes. Yes. Whenever he was balls-deep inside his little she-cat. He liked her claws, and everything else about the photographer.

"Theo, thanks for joining us this morning." Jared shook his hand, bringing him back to the present business at hand. Naomi innocuously slipped out of the living room.

"It's my pleasure. I appreciate the invitation," Theo said.

"Were you able to finish those last few items?" Jared asked his voice low to keep the conversation private.

Theo knew that Jared wanted to surprise Naomi, and before he could respond or discover if she'd accepted Jared's proposal they were interrupted.

"Sirs, breakfast is ready if you'd like to adjourn to the kitchen," Naomi said from the doorway between the living room and kitchen.

"Lead the way," Theo said. He trailed behind the couple noting the way Jared clasped Naomi's hand when they met in the doorway, and how they interacted. Jared and Naomi were like two magnets as they moved. They probably didn't even realize it. Jared's eyes followed her as she moved about the state-of-the-art kitchen. And Naomi was just as intricately in tune with Jared. Theo sat across from Jared at the round kitchen table as Naomi began serving them. He liked that they weren't eating in the formal dining room off to the right of the kitchen. He preferred the more relaxed setting.

"I hope you like it, Sir. I wasn't sure what you liked. It's an old family recipe," Naomi said.

"You cooked?" Theo asked, liking the hominess of it, noting the feminine touches at the table and in the kitchen. It was nice, although he felt the fact that he noticed it showed his age. He liked dining out as much as the next bloke, but there was something to be said for a home cooked meal. More often than not, he usually cooked for himself when he was at home and on nights when his housekeeper didn't have the time. Theo wondered if Piper cooked. He'd have to ask her, since whenever they were at her place, they were typically in her bed or playing in the dungeon.

"Yes, Sir," Naomi replied.

"She's a woman of many talents," Jared said, winking at Naomi as she filled their plates. There was a breakfast casserole of sorts, with eggs, sausage, peppers, and onions; buttery flakey croissants; and baked cinnamon apples.

"It looks amazing. Truly," Theo murmured.

"Coffee?" she asked, and the diamond ring Jared had shown him the other day flashed on her left hand.

"Yes, please. And I see congratulations are in order," Theo said, as the song *Another One Bites the Dust* played in his mind. First Declan and now Jared. Who was next? The DFC would end up being a bloody wasteland of old married couples.

"Aye, my Naomi is never getting rid of me now," Jared said, placing a kiss on the back on Naomi's hand. She blushed a becoming shade of pink.

A heated look passed between the lovebirds as Naomi sat at the table beside Jared.

"Have you decided on the date?" Theo asked as he delved into the sumptuous offerings on his plate. He damn near sighed at the first bite. Naomi was an excellent cook.

"Um, no, not yet. He just proposed last night," Naomi admitted.

"We have lots to decide. I think my mum and da would want to be there though. What would you think of having a Scottish wedding?" Jared asked.

"Maybe," Naomi said, blushing even more deeply, and then she asked Theo, "How's your breakfast? Would you like any more?"

"It's delicious, and I will say yes to second helpings. Jared's going to need to invest in longer belts and trouser sizes with your magical kitchen skills. I think you could give Mrs. Davos a run for her money. Don't tell her I said that, though, she might stop making my biscuits and scones," Theo said, his voice low, acting like it was a secret.

Naomi's musical laugh burst forth. "Thank you, and not a word, I promise."

"So, I noticed that you and Piper have been getting to know one another," Jared said, taking a sip of his coffee, and pushing his empty plate back. Theo knew the look on Jared's face, the quizzical interest and friendly demeanor. Jared tended to look out for everyone, especially the subs, which was what made him such a good Dom, and an even better owner of this island getaway. His friend tended to collect subs who needed help.

"We have," Theo admitted, warmth suffusing him at the thought of her. The way she'd looked this morning as he'd left her. His dick twitched. He hadn't wanted to leave her bed. In fact, it had taken everything inside him to pull himself from the comfort of her body. And when she'd given him her inviting little sleepy half-grin, bleeding Christ but he'd wanted to slide back under the covers and tell Jared he could sod off.

"I'm surprised," Jared replied, studying him. Theo should have expected the line of questioning.

"None more so than I, but she's an interesting woman, dedicated to her craft." Theo wanted to keep it light and didn't want to delve into his feelings for his little she-cat. He wanted her to distraction, and that was all he was comfortable with examining at the present.

Jared barked a laugh at his response and said, "You've got it bad for the little photographer. It looks good on you, Theo. It's serious, then?"

Was it? Theo had thought he was just slaking his lust, using the time away from home to satisfy his darker sexual needs. Piper was the perfect sub for him in the bedroom. She was generous, sensual, and catered to whatever fantasy he desired. But he liked her, she was funny, intelligent, and resourceful, not to mention he only had to think about her and he was sporting an erection.

It was serious? When the hell had that happened? Did he even want a serious relationship with Piper? She wasn't the easiest sub in the world, by any means, and she kept him on his toes. Then again, if she'd been a dullard, he would have already moved on by now.

Instead of giving Jared a direct answer, he deflected. "I'm not sure yet. We are enjoying each other's company, though."

That was his story and he was sticking with it.

"How are you getting her to scene with you? Like I told you before, I don't know of any Dom who has," Jared asked, his confusion prominent.

Theo tiptoed around his response. What Piper had expressed to him had been in confidence and he would not break her trust. He said, "She does have some ghosts from the past that I've been helping her work through. Granted, I'm not sure I can convince her to do a scene in the club."

"Why do you say that?"

"She was hurt, badly, and I don't know that it's the right course of action." And that was the most Theo could say without betraying Piper. It had taken him quite a bit to get her to trust him and he wouldn't damage that, not even for his friend.

"Sir, if you don't mind me saying this, but without Jared's help, and him pushing me in some of our scenes, I wouldn't have really begun healing at all. I don't know Piper or her situation, but I know I had a hard time asking for what I needed because of my past," Naomi said.

Jared's arm circled Naomi's shoulders and he kissed her temple. Theo had never seen two people more in sync with the other—except perhaps him and Piper. And wasn't that just the drop-kick to the balls he wasn't expecting this morning.

"I appreciate the insight, Naomi. I can see how lucky Jared is."

"That he is, but then again, so am I," she said, snuggling into Jared's shoulder.

"Naomi's right, my friend. If you're wanting to form a more permanent bond with Piper, you will need to push her boundaries more. Talk to her, work out the scene you want to do with her, and then see. If it crashes and burns, it does." He shrugged. "Then you go back to the drawing board."

"I'll take it into consideration," Theo said as Naomi began clearing plates off the table and refilling coffee cups. "Now, about these." He pulled his file from his briefcase. "Everything is in order, with all the specifications and moderations."

"Naomi, lass, I will need your signature on these," Jared said to Naomi, who wiped her hands on a towel and walked back to the table.

"What are they?" she asked, staring at the mound of paperwork Theo had placed on the table like it was an undiscovered creature they'd pulled from the ocean.

Jared took her hand as she sat down beside him and said, "This makes you my partner on the island should anything happen to me before we are wed. This one is the deed to the hotel, along with the majority of my possessions, a home in Scotland and the like, that I wanted to add you to… things like that."

"You made me your partner?" Naomi said, clutching her chest. There were tears in her eyes.

"You already are, lass. This just makes it formal and legal in the eyes of the law. Like I told you last night, you are my other half, and I want you with me in all things."

Naomi burst into tears. Jared pulled his sub onto his lap. Theo turned his head, giving the couple privacy, but he still heard Naomi say, "I love you, Sir, so much. I don't know what I did to deserve you, I just—"

"I didn't mean to make you cry, little one. I just want you cared for in all things."

Jared was truly a lucky man. But it made Theo think about Piper. Seeing Jared with Naomi, the protective way in which he comforted her, and the joy in him as he did so, made Theo wonder. Did he want to explore more with Piper? Should he attempt a scene at the club with her?

With Jared and Naomi sitting side by side, Theo explained in detail each document to Naomi. She had a keen mind and refused to sign things blindly, so Theo answered every question she had about what she was signing, insisting on reading every one before she put her signature on it. Jared had his secretary join them to notarize each document. By the time they had finished, it was midday. Theo left the happy couple and headed into Jared's office.

Jared had given him the conference area to make his own, and he had a work station set up at the far end, with his laptop, a smattering of files and a fresh pot of coffee, thanks to Jared's secretary. The estate matters for Jared were finally complete. Theo arranged a file of the signed documents that would go to Jared, one to Naomi, one that he always liked to keep on file for his clients as a backup that he would scan and save in digital format at his offsite storage facility, and then a fourth and final copy that he would file with the courts in London. Since Jared was technically a UK citizen, he would file them upon his return to London, even with the island being an international business.

With the McTavish estate documents finished, Theo moved on to completing the rest of the legal documents for the island.

Theo was undertaking the task of compiling the hotel's company by-laws, updating them with all the additions and modifications Jared had made and was planning to make in the future. He was also establishing a Meeting Minutes document that Jared, or most likely, his secretary, would need to complete whenever the island board met, even though they did the bulk of their meetings online. The paperwork also included the operating agreement for the board of trustees, and updates to the non disclosure agreements, especially since Jenna was leaving the island and they were expanding to include members from other clubs. With Jenna's departure, Jared wanted some updates made to the present employee agreement too, which Theo thought was wise as well.

There was an updated business plan, memorandum of understanding, online terms of use, online privacy policy, and an apostille, what with this being an international company.

Theo worked through lunch, opting to plow through the stack. He made considerable progress, since he had already conducted an assessment of the island and made lists. He was famous for his lists at Apex. And through it all, as he typed up the information, composing each form in his pre-made templates, he pondered the conundrum Piper presented.

Did he want more with her? Perhaps to see her again after they both left the island?

Yes, he did. More than he was comfortable with. She made him ache for more time with her. What did that mean for his life? Distance was a factor. He wouldn't leave Jacob, not for anyone. So where would that leave him trying to maintain a relationship with a woman who lived half a world away?

It didn't. Maybe he could entice her to visit upon occasion, but could they really have a relationship, or would they just be each other's occasional fuck buddy? Although that idea also had merit because the woman, even with her damn claws, made him hotter than the island at midday. He craved her touch, her submission.

But she was also holding back from him. She had studiously avoided the topic of her panic attacks. As much as he had attempted to put it from his mind, he couldn't ignore that she had them. Nor could he ignore the fact that she didn't trust him enough to tell him the truth about what had happened to her.

He had a gut feeling and was suspicious, but he didn't want to make assumptions. Maybe Jared's fiancée had been right, maybe he did need to push her boundaries a bit more. He was a freaking Master, and she had him so wrapped up that he was questioning himself. Of course he needed to push her boundaries more. Blast it all, she'd done well in the restaurant, remarkably so, perhaps tonight they could take it a step further. Theo was a firm believer in taking happiness where one could find it. He would do it. He never backed away from a challenge. Maybe that was why she enticed him so much.

Did he want more from Piper? Absolutely. She thrilled him. She was a feisty as hell sub and got his blood pumping any time she was in his vicinity. Every time he had her beneath him, feeling the sweet clasp of her body around him, he felt like he was home. He rubbed his chest at the revelation. Would she agree to see him after they left the island? Did she want more from him? That was the real question.

The first step was to press past her fear of submitting outside of the bedroom. This was not just about her fears but her willingness to trust him completely. If she didn't trust him, they didn't have a relationship, and were in fact just scratching an itch. Going on instinct, Theo contacted the club and reserved one of the alcoves for that evening. Tonight, he would break past her barriers, get her to trust him with the rest of her story.

Knowing Piper, she would likely kick up a stink at first, but with some cajoling on his part, Theo believed he could entice her, make her come around to his way of thinking.

He worked until it was time to meet Piper for dinner. At quarter to the hour, he saved and closed out of his documents to resume working on them in the morning. He wondered for the hundredth time if their relationship had entered serious territory. Would she commit and agree to his proposal?

It was balls to the wall time. He would know soon enough whether they were on the same page or not.

And if she wasn't, what then?

Chapter 11

Theo waited until they had finished dinner to broach the deeper subject matters. Piper was wearing a skin tight, aquamarine dress that hugged every blessed curve on her body and fell to mid-thigh. He'd been sporting wood all throughout dinner, making it difficult to focus when he would prefer avoiding the delicate subject matter and jump to losing himself in her welcoming heat instead.

Piper's normal exuberance had been muted throughout dinner. She was the one who finally broke the silence, turning her blue gaze his way, unable to keep the concern from her expression. She asked, "Is something wrong, Sir? You've been distant all day today. If you don't want to see me anymore, I'll understand. You only wanted me for this week and—"

Theo sighed over his lack of communication. That wasn't what he'd intended. He said, "Piper, that's not it at all. I apologize. Today was a bit of a bear with work. As you might have heard, Jared got engaged last night. Some of the items I've been overseeing this week had to do with a few things he wanted put in place for his new fiancée. That's why I had the early breakfast meeting. And I kept you up rather late last night, and wanted to let you rest a bit."

"Oh. I just assumed when you didn't, um, when we didn't have sex this morning, that you were getting bored with me." She gave him a caustic stare, almost daring him to discount her statement.

"Bored? With you?" He shook his head. "That's not going to happen anytime soon. It's taken all my self-control to keep my hands off you in that dress. And the only reason I haven't bent you over this table is because I have plans for you tonight. Plus, there is something I wanted to discuss with you. How would you feel about extending our relationship past the island? I like you, Piper. I care for you, and I think you might have feelings for me too. I want to see more of you. How would you feel about visiting me in London? Or letting me visit you in Santa Barbara upon occasion?"

Her face had transformed as he had spoken, shifting from a defensive she-cat ready to gouge his eyes out to a softened expression, with a strawberry blush spreading over her tanned skin. Theo had really mucked it up with her today. He should have been more forthcoming before he left her that morning. It reminded him of just how long he'd only had himself and his worries to consider on a daily basis. Adding a submissive to his life outside of the club was new territory for him, as well. Even Piper's body had relaxed, and a hesitant smile had formed on her lips. "I would like that, Sir, very much so."

Pleasure spread through him at her response. The thought of taking her to his bed, his private dungeon, having her greet him properly when he arrived home from work, was a heady aphrodisiac to his system. He threaded his fingers through hers and said, "I'm glad, Piper. I'm looking forward to seeing where you live."

"I don't have a dungeon or anything, but I do have a pool and hot tub, so it's a tradeoff."

"We'll just have to improvise. Besides, I do. When you to come to London, I'll show you. Are you still working on your meal? Because I have something I would like us to try this evening."

"No, I'm finished. So, you don't want to…" She waved toward the table.

Infinitely pleased with the direction in which the night had headed, Theo shook his head. At her crestfallen look, he reassured her and said, "Not to worry, it doesn't mean I don't want you. In fact, I have every intention of eating your sweet pussy many times over tonight. But I have another place in mind I would like us to try. The real question is, do you trust me?"

"Yes, I do trust you, Sir," she said, her voice full of sincerity. The faith shining in her gaze humbled him. He wouldn't let her down but would guide her gently tonight.

"Thank you. Come with me, it's time we begin." He stood and tossed his napkin on the table, then helped her stand. Piper rose without hesitation, gripping his hand tightly and showing absolutely no fear. All good signs in his estimation that she trusted him implacably, which he would need to use as he pushed her past her comfort zone this evening. Theo pulled her into his arms and she slid into them willingly. His heart squeezed at her easy compliance. He brushed his lips against hers, tasting the wine she'd had with dinner, and her distinct flavor. Lust battled with his desire to help her heal. There was a part of Theo that would prefer to keep her bounty all to himself, that would like to forgo the club, splay her back over the table, and bury himself inside her.

But instead of giving in to the temptation her succulent body presented, he released her lips, regretfully, and steered her out of the restaurant to the lift. There would be plenty of time for him to slake himself on her bounty. For the next hour or so, it was about Piper, and helping her overcome her fear. At the elevator bank, he kept her focus on him, toying with her fingers, teasing the outline of her nipples through her dress. It worked because she didn't pay attention to the button he pressed inside the elevator, but leaned her head against his shoulder instead. And even though there was a part of him that worried she would castigate him for not explaining what he had planned, Theo knew Piper would flatly refuse him.

He believed that if he could get her into the club and have her focus on him, instead of worrying all the way, it might circumvent her anxiety and allow her to do a scene. He had made the right decision where she was concerned, on all fronts. There was infinitely more between them, much more than a simple week could uncover.

Theo imagined taking her to his private dungeon and living out every single fantasy he could dream up. Something told him she would be on board with it all. Hell, he could see himself introducing her to Jacob at some point. Since he and his ex-wife had split, there'd never been a woman important enough he had even considered introducing to his son. Piper truly was amazing.

The elevator doors dinged as they slid open and music blasted the couple. The club was hopping tonight. It appeared that Jared and Naomi were having an impromptu celebration. Trepidation wiggled into Theo; of all the nights for the club to look like a spectator's sport and be jam packed, it had to be tonight. He almost aborted the mission, since the place was crowded with bodies as they got off the elevator.

"What's this, Sir? Why are we here?" Piper glanced at him accusingly, fear swimming in her gaze. Her body was no longer pliant against his but had turned so rigid it was like she was made of stone.

"I reserved one of the alcoves for us tonight. I think it's time we attempt a scene here, don't you? I have something simple planned and we will use the blindfold again. I will be with you the whole time, walking you through it," he challenged her as her hand trembled in his. A part of him wanted to sweep her up, protect her from the demons she needed to face, and carry her away from the club. But he knew if she didn't confront it, she'd be running from living to the fullest her entire life.

Piper panted, her breathing rough, and she glanced around the bustling club. The pulse in her neck fluttered and she returned her fearful gaze toward his and said, "I'm not sure, Sir. The restaurant is one thing, but this, do we have to? Please, can't we just go back to my place, or even yours tonight?"

Theo caressed the side of her face, trying to calm her anxiety. "I will be with you every step of the way. It will be just like we've practiced at the restaurant these last few days. I don't want you to focus on anyone but me while we are here, okay? And I will not leave your side the entire time. I believe in you, Piper, that you can do this."

Piper searched his face, fear clouding her visage, her body ramrod straight as tremors wracked her slight frame. He was about to abort, worried that he had pushed her too far. Then she nodded with a shaky breath and said, "I trust you."

Pride, and another emotion he wasn't ready to examine, flooded through him. She was incredible in her bravery. Now it was up to him to ensure the scene went off without a hitch. He guided her through the crowd to the alcove he'd reserved. In the eight by eight space stood a medical table, with the back raised at an angle and metal stirrups. Theo only planned to restrain her and give her oral. For this first time, he wanted a scene that was simple and brought her pleasure. They could save the more complicated scenes for when her trust in him was implicit and they'd moved past her fear.

Inside the alcove, he ordered, "Disrobe for me, please. Then bring your gorgeous ass over here."

Theo patted the black leather seat. She nodded and did as he requested, her fingers shaking slightly. He kept his gaze trained on her as he stripped out of his dress shirt and tie, so he would catch the first sign of distress if her anxiety and panic got the better of her. He noted that the leather restraints were already at the station as he had requested.

When she was nude, he held out a hand, drawing her over to the medical table. He helped her up and noticed her eyes were wide with fear.

"Relax, Piper, deep breaths. For our scene, I'm going to restrain you, then eat your pretty little pussy. That's it, nothing more. I want you to focus on me and the pleasure I'm giving you, understood? And remember, use your safeword, love, if you need it. Eyes on me."

She nodded, biting her lower lip, and drew a deep breath in through her nose. She kept her gaze trained on him and he waited to press further until her body relaxed slightly. Good. It meant she was letting go of her fear and putting more emphasis on her trust in him. Then he fit a black blindfold over her eyes. At the last second, her gaze darted to the crowd forming beyond the velvet rope of their alcove.

Damnit.

That was the last thing he wanted her to focus on. He brushed his lips against hers, wanting to override any panic on her part. Her lips were like ice as he kissed her, warming them with his caress.

"Focus on me, Piper," Theo spoke to her in soothing tones. "I love how wet you get when my tongue is plunging inside your pussy, how it weeps for my touch."

He attached her wrists to the side of the table. "And I adore the little noises you make in the back of your throat just when you are about to come. It's sexy as hell."

Then he fit her legs in the stirrups, positioning them so that they were bent at the knee and spread wide open. And through it all, he talked to her, telling her what a good submissive she was and more.

In the alcove beside them, Sherry was in the middle of a torrid three-way with her Doms. The trio were now screwing on the sawhorse. Nick and Patrick were rather vocal in their pleasure as they pumped inside Sherry. They were loud enough that even the club music didn't overshadow their grunts. The song currently playing on the hidden speakers was a thumping bass number. Laughter erupted near the center dais. Then Piper went rigid, struggling against her bonds.

Tears were leaking from her beneath her blindfold and panic erupted inside Theo.

"Relax, Piper, focus on me and the pleasure."

If anything, at his words, she became more agitated, fighting against her restraints, but she wasn't using her safeword. He reached for her, attempting to soothe her with his touch. But when he stroked her face, Piper let loose with a blood-curdling scream.

"Piper," he yelled. He tore the blindfold off and Piper gave him a thousand-yard stare as she fiercely struggled against her bonds. Fucking hell, she was having an attack. Her gaze didn't even register that she could see him as her distressed movements increased against her bonds.

Jared stepped into the alcove. "What the fuck happened?"

"Help me get her out of the restraints. She's having a panic attack," Theo said, cursing under his breath. He and Jared undid the bonds, removing the smooth leather from her trembling form. She was shaking so violently, Theo's own panic escalated. He'd pushed her too far. The moment he'd spied the full gathering, he should have canceled the scene immediately. And now he was worried that she wasn't coming out of her trance-like state. Horror clouded her face. Fast and furious tears streamed down her cheeks.

A warm blanket was handed to him and he wrapped it around her shoulders. "I've got you, love, it's just me, you'll be fine. Come back to me, Piper. You're safe. Piper, can you hear me?"

Picking her up, he left the alcove and settled on one of the nearby couches that Jared had made other club attendees vacate. The music started up again with a softer, more seductive song.

"Get them further back," Theo snarled at Jared, needing to create a safe space for Piper. Jared shooed the crowd away, getting the other DMs to form a barrier and protective circle around Theo and Piper.

"Come on, love, follow the sound of my voice and come back to me. I'm here, you're safe," Theo crooned. Little by little, as he murmured to her, gently coaxing her, her struggles diminished with the sound of his voice.

Jared knelt down beside the couch as Piper sputtered and gasped, drawing in a full, deep breath. Thank god.

"That's it, Piper, you're safe. Deep breaths, love." Theo stroked a hand down her back.

"Are you all right, lass?" Jared asked, searching her face. Theo knew he'd messed up tonight, and so did Jared. But he wasn't concerned about any punishment from the DFC, only worried about Piper and ensuring she was okay. He'd deal with the rest when the time came.

She sat rigid in Theo's arms but nodded at Jared, tears flowing down her cheeks, and said, "Yes, Sir. I just need to leave. I can't stay in the club."

"I'll get her home," Theo said. She was his damn sub, and he'd prefer it if everyone backed the hell off so he could care for her. The scene had gone horribly awry but he would fix it.

Jared, nearly a decade his junior, glared furiously at him and snapped, "I will make sure she's unharmed before she leaves my club. I don't give a flying fuck whether you are a Master or not, after the scream I heard, it's not up to you."

Theo knew Jared was only looking out for Piper. And, in truth, if positions were reversed, he'd want the same. As much as it galled him to do so, he conceded with a slight nod of compliance. Theo's concern in this entire fucked up night was Piper.

"I'm fine. It wasn't Theo's fault, Jared. I just want to go. I need to go, please don't keep me here." Piper sobbed and buried her face in Theo's shoulder. He held her close, attempting to soothe her with his touch, stroking her back.

"Call me if you need anything, lass," Jared said gently to Piper before his irate green gaze whipped to Theo. "You're free to leave. We'll talk tomorrow morning."

After the uproar he had caused, Theo merely nodded. He would be fine with whatever disciplinary measures Jared and the rest of the DFC members lobbed at him. Tonight was his fault. Piper's panic attack was his fault. In his desire to make a deeper connection with Piper—and, he had to admit, reinforce his skills as a Master—he had pushed his little sub too far. Assuaging his guilt was the least of his concerns. Piper's well-being came first, above all else.

Theo carried her out of the club. His heart broke as she trembled in his arms. He prayed that he hadn't done too much damage and would have given nearly everything he had to rewind the evening, back to before they'd entered the club.

Holding her in his arms, he drove them back to her lodgings. Theo carried her inside, not stopping until they were seated on the leather couch. He cradled her body, holding her close.

"Why?" Piper cried into her hands. "Why did you make me do that?"

"I'm sorry, love. I arrogantly thought it was time to test your boundaries a bit more. You'd done so well each time in the restaurant, I thought—"

"But I told you from the start of this thing that I couldn't do public scenes. I told you that I don't do them for a reason. Do you know why?" she sobbed, shoving his arms away and scrambling off his lap until she had put the coffee table between them. He felt every inch of the distance between them, the wall she was erecting. Piper paced the floor, her movements jerky.

"No, I don't. Why don't you explain it to me, then. Bloody hell, I wasn't trying to hurt you. I'd sooner lop off an arm than do that. I was trying to help you, you have to believe that. I'm so very sorry that you had an attack tonight and that it was my doing, that I pushed you too far. But you survived and came out of it."

"And what happens if I don't surface from an attack? Did you even for a second consider that, big guy? Let's get something straight here. Just because we've had a few good fucks, doesn't mean you understand anything about me. I can't do public scenes and be the perfect little submissive. Seeing those people surround the scene area and hearing the laughter put me right back into the nightmare I can't outrun."

"How can I help you heal if you don't tell me what happened?" he said, rising, his own temper boiling over after the strain of the evening.

She gestured with her hands as she paced the room and shouted, "You want to know? Fine. Fourteen years ago, I was visiting Kenya. I was hungry to score photos for *National Geographic* and a few other magazines to really make my mark. followed a young boy into his village, thinking I would capture the photo of a lifetime. I did. And it's a picture I can't destroy because its imprinted on the very fabric of my soul." She inhaled a shuddering breath and continued, "In the village, there was a group of men, sitting near the communal fire. They'd been drinking. And they decided as a group to rape me. I wasn't fast enough to get away. There were six of them. They held me down in the grass, and one by one, they raped me. I can still recall every man's face, what their laughter sounded like, the smell of the smoke from the communal fire. The agony as they forced their way inside me. There are parts of me that died that day. And I almost did die. When they had finished and passed out from the drink, I crawled away, bleeding, barely conscious. As luck would have it, I stumbled across a Doctors Without Borders campsite two miles away. They saved my life that night. So, ask me again why I can't do public scenes."

It was so much worse than he had assumed. Theo wished he could take away all the hurt and suffering she'd been through. He wished he could have five minutes alone with each of those fuckers who'd hurt her. The only thing he could do was offer her comfort, prove that he didn't think less of her because of the terror she'd gone through. As horrified as he was by her story, he'd never been in awe of anyone so much in his life. Theo sought to close the distance between them and approached her, moving around the coffee table. "Piper, love, I'm so sorry. I didn't mean to hurt you tonight. Just—"

She lobbed a book at his head and he ducked just in the nick of time as she screeched, her voice filled with so much pain, "Get out. I don't want to see you. Just leave."

Piper scurried out of the living room, heading directly into the bathroom. She slammed the door shut. He heard the flip of the lock as he advanced across the room and then pounded his fist on the door. "Piper, let's talk this through. I won't ask anything of you tonight but your forgiveness."

"Just leave, Theo. If you want me to consider forgiving you, I need space, I need time. Please leave." She sobbed brokenly and his heart ached for her.

Theo stared at the door. He knew he had fucked up monumentally. Would she ever forgive him? Her cries pierced his soul and he had never felt so helpless in all his life. Short of breaking down the door, all he could do was wait her out and pray that he hadn't ruined everything between them. Theo would give her tonight, do as she asked, and give her the space she begged him for. Perhaps then they could mend fences in the morning and he could seek atonement for his epic blunder this evening.

"I will leave my number on the fridge. Call me if you need anything. I'm sorry, Piper," Theo murmured and backed away from the bathroom door. Her muffled sobs would live with him for a long time to come. On his way out, he scribbled his number on a piece of paper and put it up on her fridge. Then he let himself out of the villa.

He'd royally screwed the pooch on this one. When he'd seen how crowded the club was this evening and sensed her fear, he should have backed off. And now she might never speak to him again. He stormed inside his villa and headed directly to the fridge. He yanked a beer out, nearly ripping the cap off, and swallowed a long draught before he noticed that his personal cell phone on the counter was flashing that there was a message. Just as he reached for the device, his ex-wife's name flashed on his screen as she called.

It was barely ten on the island, which meant it was the middle of the night in London. Theo answered, "Diane, what's going on?"

"It's Jacob. He was in an accident. He's in the hospital and in surgery right now, but—"

"I'm on my way. Text me the hospital info and I will be there as soon as I can get a flight to Heathrow," Theo said, his heart lodging itself in his throat. Terror unlike anything he'd known before swamped him. He couldn't lose Jacob.

"Okay, I will. Have a safe flight and keep me updated on your arrival," Diane said. He could hear the fear and worry in her voice.

"Likewise, on our son." Theo ended the call and immediately sprang into action. He withdrew his work cell from his back pocket and saw the numerous missed calls from Diane. He'd set the ringer to silent for his evening with Piper, never imagining how fucked up the night would become.

He dialed the one person he knew could help get him home quickly.

"Theo, so help me, if you've harmed her even more, I will personally beat the shit out of you," Jared snarled through the receiver.

"Jared, yes, I know you will. Listen, I didn't call to talk about

Piper. My son is in the hospital. I need to get to London as soon as possible. Do you have one of Declan's jets handy?" Theo asked. If there was ever a time he would use his position and sway at Apex, it was now.

"That I do, and it's at your disposal. I will start making arrangements and come get you myself to take you to the airstrip. I'll have Mary get your things from the office as well."

Relief flooded Theo and he said, "Thanks, J. I owe you one."

"Get yourself packed and I will be back with you in a flash," Jared said, disconnecting the call.

Theo packed his clothes and belongings in record time. A pair of lace panties floated on top of his things as he was about to close his suitcase. Piper. Bugger it, he didn't have time to break through her defenses right now and get her to listen to why he had to leave tonight. Damnit, he had way too many fires to extinguish. There was no time to reach her when she wouldn't even let him in the door. Theo would have to call Piper from London and explain what had happened. As for the rest, their relationship, he would deal with it later. Worry for Jacob was clouding his judgement.

As Theo snapped his suitcase shut, Jared arrived at his villa in his jeep. Theo rushed out of the lodge, shoving his luggage in the back where he spied his briefcase.

"The private jet should be at the airstrip in ten minutes, give or take. Don't worry about anything else, I will drive you. They should be able to get you to London and your boy."

Theo didn't look back as they sped away from his lodge. They passed the turnoff to Piper's place and his heart ached that he was leaving her like this. It was another item to add to his list of things to make amends for. Jared got him to the airstrip just as the jet landed.

Jared greeted the pilot as Theo lugged his belongings onto the plane. Once he had his baggage stowed, he went to the airplane door, shook Jared's hand and said, "Thanks for everything, J. If you would, please make sure Piper's all right. I will check on her as well, once I get everything sorted with Jacob. She's fine now, but keep an eye on her for me, will you?"

"You know I will. I'm going to talk to her about what happened. Procedure and all," Jared warned him.

That didn't concern Theo other than he knew Piper was fragile at the moment, and said, "Be gentle with her. She's been through more than you know, and don't be surprised if she doesn't tell you everything."

Jared gave Theo an assessing glance and said, "Got it. She's in good hands. Let me know how Jacob is doing"

"I know. I will," Theo said, and then Jared loped down the stairs, leaving him on board the jet. At the pilot's order, he sat down and fastened his seatbelt. He hated leaving Piper like this, he thought as the door closed and engines revved to life.

One problem at a time. His son came first in everything. Once Theo was certain Jacob was okay, then he would tackle the issues with Piper.

Chapter 12

A t the slamming of her back door, Piper dissolved onto her bathroom floor. Tears streamed down her face, blinding her vision as she grappled with an unending tide of grief. She was glad Theo had left so he didn't hear more of her sobs. Tonight had been awful, going from one extreme, brimming with hope and excitement, to having her nightmare unleashed in front of everyone on the island. All those people at the club now knew about her weakness. Shame bombarded her and she tried to breathe. The fact that Jared had felt the need to check on her meant only one thing; her episode had been beyond bad.

Maybe if she hadn't spent the majority of her day worrying that Theo was losing interest, she wouldn't have spiraled into an attack. All because he hadn't woken her up for an early morning tumble before he'd left for the day. That tiny hiccup to their new routine had sent her spinning. How pathetic was she? Not even a week ago, she would have laughed if someone had told her she'd spend a day mooning over a man.

For all her bravado, fear controlled her life when it came to relationships. Even though Theo had said he wanted to continue their relationship, the disruption she'd felt when he didn't do a mini-scene with her in the restaurant had added fuel to the doubts which had plagued her throughout the day.

So when they'd waltzed into the club, she'd already been on a razor's edge. The two glasses of wine she'd imbibed at dinner had removed the rest of her defenses, and voila: a recipe for disaster. As Theo led her to the alcove, the club had morphed before her eyes and become too bright, too loud, with far too many people. Her anxiety, already near panic levels, had skyrocketed. She'd felt like the walls were closing in on her. Then the grunts from some of the Doms in sessions, combined with the frivolity and laughter all around them, had undermined her ability to fight through her panic. Before she had a chance to stop it, she was in the midst of her nightmare.

She'd call her therapist in the morning. Maybe she needed her meds checked, or maybe she really was destined to live a lonely life. Both of her attacks had come because of her relationship with Theo, which meant she was being foolhardy and obstinate in her desire to continue seeing him.

Because, as much as she had tried not to, she'd fallen for Theo. Even now, a part of her wished she hadn't sent him away so that she could go curl up in his arms and let him help carry her burdens. She was so pathetic and desperate for someone to love that she forgot the most important lesson out of everything she'd learned in life.

Choices had consequences.

How could she have been so foolish, falling for him and imagining building a life with him? All she'd done was erect castles in the air. That dream life wasn't real. And with her handicap, it wasn't sustainable. Deep down, she'd known that truth and had ignored the warnings sounding in her mind. She couldn't be a normal submissive and hope that a Dom would forgive her her shortcomings. That wasn't how the real world worked.

In her heart, she knew Theo hadn't meant to push her toward an attack. He'd been wonderful in his attempts to heal her. She wasn't angry with him in the slightest. It was her fault. She'd hidden how bad her sexual assault had been from him until it was too late. As their relationship had progressed this week, she should have told him, trusted him with the truth. Given him the entire story so that he understood the severity of her assault, and then allowed him the chance to digest the breadth and scope of what he had to contend with in having her as his submissive. Piper knew she wasn't easy. Maybe, if she had been more honest and open with him, tonight never would have happened.

If she was angry with anyone, it was herself. But he knew now. She wasn't certain what that meant for them or their relationship. Maybe eventually, when she felt sure enough of them, if they were going to see each other past this week, they could try again. Perhaps when she felt their relationship was on solid footing, she would agree to a public scene as she became more confident in their relationship.

There were parts of her rape her psyche had shielded her from, for which she was glad, because those blank areas allowed her to function like a normal human being. But having lots of people around during a scene brought that night back in full surround sound. The pain, the multitude of hands grabbing at her, holding her down as she struggled to escape. She'd barely fled with her life.

Piper felt hollowed out when she finally emerged from the bathroom into the lonely expanse of her villa. Chilled to the bone, she bundled up in her most comfortable pajamas and curled up in bed under a mound of covers. It might be eighty something degrees outside but she was freezing. For Piper, it felt like it was twenty degrees and she couldn't seem to get warm enough. Then she smelled him—Theo—on the pillow beside her. The one he'd used the last few nights. She tugged it over and sniffed it. The cotton linen carried the barest hint of his scent, amber and cedar, and just him. She buried her face in the pillow and inhaled. Her body relaxed by degrees as she laid her head upon his pillow, allowing his essence to surround her.

Strange that it took his scent to calm her. Eventually she drifted asleep. She'd have to remember to tell him... in the morning.

AFTER TEN HOURS of uninterrupted sleep, Piper awoke marginally refreshed and with a new sense of purpose. First of all, she had to apologize to Theo. Last night had been a disaster. They had each played their parts in the mess and she had handled her end poorly. She realized that now; it was just that when she had an episode, it tended to skew her emotions so they were all out of whack. It meant her reactions to stimuli tended to get overblown. Only by talking about last night, and where each of them had bungled things, could she and Theo venture on to the topic—or even consider the possibility—of continuing their relationship past the week on the island. Piper steeled her heart for disappointment. He might have changed his mind last night after learning the truth of her nightmare. She'd be a fool not to prepare herself for the possibility.

Then, that afternoon, she had a meeting with Jared to review the brochure mock-ups she'd created with all the images she'd photographed. Piper was confident that the finished product would exceed his expectations. There was an overabundance of material on the island, what with its natural beauty and what Jared had created with the resort. She'd hoped for material to add to her gallery in Santa Barbara, but with all the shots she'd gotten, it was likely going to be an entire show. This job had been an absolute gold mine, which thrilled her. She always strived for excellence in her business, and it appeared she would end up with so much more than she had bargained for.

Before she left the villa, she called her therapist. Her office wasn't open but Piper went ahead and left a message. Dr. Caroline Winter's schedule was on west coast time. It was barely six in the morning there and would be hours before she made it into the office. Caroline tended to make exceptions for Piper's travel schedule, so if Piper needed a phone session, she made herself available. With two attacks in such a short time span, if her previous pattern held, Piper knew that a third would be on its way.

She hated the weakness, always feeling like there was this giant anvil swinging on a rope above her head, ready to snap at a moment's notice to crush her life into smithereens. The problem was that anything could set it off. There wasn't just one trigger. Years ago, during a shoot in Rocky Mountain National Park, there had been campers innocuously roasting marshmallows a few campsites down, and whammy, just the scent of a campfire made Piper have an attack. That didn't happen all the time, but it had in that instance. Last night, it had been the laughter and all the people in the club.

She was a total nut job, who had fallen for a not-so-stuffy Brit. She was a grown ass woman and had lost her heart faster than a tween at a boy band concert.

Piper took extra time to wash the grime, tears, and sleep away in the shower. She added a bit of color to her face, with some bronzer to hide her hollowed out appearance, then a dollop of mascara to her lashes. There, she thought, much better—although her eyes still carried a haunted sheen to them. Even ten hours of sleep hadn't been enough to wipe away the strain of another episode. When Piper finally emerged from the villa, it was mid-morning. The sun beamed down through leafy green fronds and palm trees. The air was rife with humidity, puffy thick clouds circling the lone island mountain peak. With her camera equipment and computer in tow, she opted to take the golf cart.

There weren't merely butterflies fluttering around in her belly but giant bats flapping their leathery wings. And as Theo's villa came into view, their wings accelerated to hummingbird speeds, along with her heart rate. Would he forgive her for last night? And did he still wish to continue their relationship past the stint on the island? Or did he just want to forget the whole thing and end it now?

She parked near the elevator and his cart, then rode the lift to the unit. The silver doors slid open with a silent ding. With her heart in her throat, Piper entered.

"Theo, are you here? Sir? I'd like to apologize." She glanced around the open format of the villa, nearly identical to hers but with some different BDSM equipment in the mini-dungeon area. It was odd how the two of them had automatically gravitated toward her place and not his. He'd spent more nights with her than he had in his room.

That was the tiny sliver of hope she held on to as she searched the place. The bathroom door was shut. He had to be in there. Perhaps he was in the shower. The distinct sound of running water reached her ears, and she smiled. If all else failed, she could always join him. The man seemed to be putty in her hands once she was naked.

Probably getting a late start as well, after last night. Unless he was in there with someone else. Oh, god, please don't let that be the case. She could handle his distance. She couldn't deal with seeing him with another sub. He'd never promised exclusivity.

With a whispered prayer that she wouldn't find him with another woman, she pushed the bathroom door open and said, "Theo?"

"Ah! Sweet heavens, you scared me," Jared's pretty, petite sub, Naomi, said, clutching at her chest. The dark-haired beauty pressed a yellow-gloved fist to her heart, clutching a scrubbing brush in her other hand. She held it like a sword ready to fend off an attack.

Jared's submissive was the last person Piper had expected to find in Theo's villa. Although, perhaps she was just cleaning it for him. It looked like even though the owner had fallen head over heels for Naomi, she wasn't a gold-digger, and had kept her job. Good for her. As for Theo, most likely he was already in the office. Not a big deal, Piper was the one who had gotten the late start.

"Sorry about that, I didn't realize you were here. I was trying to find Theo. Have you seen him?" Piper said.

"It's fine. Jared does it to me all the time at home. He thinks it's a hoot. I can't believe he didn't tell you. Theo left the island last night and went back to London," Naomi said, shutting off the water in the shower.

"He what? Why? When?" The room began to spin. The sudden, swift agony of abandonment lanced through her. Theo had deserted her. Piper had to keep herself from hyper-ventilating.

Naomi's dark gaze studied her as she explained, "I'm really not sure, I'm sorry. Jared helped him leave. We had just finished a session and I tend to be barely conscious afterwards—among other things. So I didn't hear the majority of their conversation. But it sounded urgent."

Dread settled like a lead weight in the pit of her stomach. There was only one reason she could surmise why Theo had left last night. Because of Piper. The last vestiges of hope she'd had for her future were decimated in the blink of an eye. She'd been too much for him. Theo had left her. She had shown him her scars and personal demons, and proved how unlovable she really was. No man wanted a woman like her, and no Dom would ever settle for a submissive who couldn't perform a scene.

"Thank you. I will leave you to your work," she murmured,

clearing her throat, fighting tears and an all-consuming grief a her heart ripped into a million pieces.

"Are you all right, Piper? I know you and I don't really know each other well, but if you need someone to talk to, I'm here, and I'm a good listener."

Piper blinked back her tears and plastered a fake smile on her face at Naomi's offer. It was very sweet of her. She could see wh Jared loved her so much. Except, Piper knew precisely why The had vacated the island. After last night, it didn't come as surprise. How pathetic was that? She'd expected it, known dee down that no man, no matter how stalwart and steadfast, woul stick around when they discovered who she truly was, and real ized the fact that her broken pieces couldn't be mended like jigsaw puzzle.

"Thank you. I might take you up on that. Could you tel Jared that I'm not feeling well and that I will meet with hin tomorrow morning to go over the brochure?"

"Certainly. And please don't hesitate to call me if you nee anything."

Piper nodded, needing to escape the offered comfort. As i was, she was plugging her fingers in the dam and it was about to blow. Instead of taking more photos, Piper raced back to he villa. She barely reached her bathroom before she lost th contents of her breakfast. Nerves and stress descended upon he form until she was dry heaving into the commode. Tear streamed down her face. She curled on the bathroom floo against the cool tiles and felt her heart bleed out onto the floor. I was over and done.

Piper cried as she hadn't in an age. She cried for the potentia of what they might have been, for the joy and pleasure he' brought into her life. Her own defects made it so much worse She sobbed as the shock of his abandonment sank in. As he tears slowed, a boiling, festering rage built.

Damn him.

He didn't have the balls to tell her in person but had taken the coward's route. How dare he make her feel for him and then leave the way he had? Was he that unfeeling? What she wouldn't give to let him have a piece of her mind. This was exactly why she didn't get involved with Doms. They stripped away your defenses, then let you crash and burn when they deemed you unworthy of their time and effort.

Piper glanced at her reflection as she brushed her teeth. She looked every inch the crazy lady. Ruddy tear marks, splotchy red cheeks, and her eyes were over bright. She splashed water on her face, to rinse some of the salt of her tears away. When she was certain her stomach had settled enough that she could leave the bathroom, she trudged to the kitchen for some water. On the fridge, she spied Theo's handwritten note with his phone number on it.

Anger, shame, and grief all rose up to strangle her airways. She took measured, deep breaths. Piper couldn't run from the fact that she had hurt him as well by not being honest from the get go. She should have told him the whole truth and not given him an edited version of it. Her mistake: one she had no intention of repeating.

Before she had time to talk herself out of it, she dialed the number and called him. His voicemail answered, "This is Theodore Brown, lead solicitor with Apex Industries. Leave a brief message, and I will get back to you straight away. Cheerio."

"Theo, it's Piper. I can't believe you pulled such a dick move and left the island the way you did. I'm sorry about the way I acted last night. I realize you were only trying to help me and I apologize that I took my fear out on you. You didn't need to leave the island to prove your point. I understand that you never want to hear from me after this, but I needed to apologize for my part in it. I am more sorry than you know that I kept the truth from you. These past few days with you, thank you for those, Sir. Please forgive me, I—" And then his voicemail cut her off.

Love you.

She sniffed as a fresh bout of tears threatened to fall. Her cell phone rang and for a brief second, hope stuttered back to life, only to be dashed when she spied her therapist's name on the screen.

"Caroline, thank you for calling me back."

"It's what I'm here for. I have an hour. Talk to me, tell me about each of your episodes. Then we can figure out what triggered you and work out an action plan."

Piper took a bottle of water she had pulled from the fridge and settled into the living room chaise. Caroline was the only person—well, in addition to Theo now—who knew the whole story about the night she was raped. Caroline knew everything about her. She knew things her mom and siblings didn't know. They just thought Piper had gotten sick and had a bad trip.

She had no reservations telling Caroline about Theo. Caroline knew that Piper was a submissive and in the lifestyle. Over the next hour, Piper poured her heart out, detailing the two occurrences, and talking about Theo. She had to tell someone. She wasn't a cold fish.

"That's quite a trip. Okay, I want you to resume your daily mantras. Then I want you in here when you get back from your trip. We might need to discuss upping your medication dosage. And if you have another attack in the meantime, call me. You have my cell for emergencies, okay?"

"Thanks, Caroline. I'm going to try and wrap up my business here tomorrow and get home."

"Great. I'll leave it with my secretary to fit you in. And Piper, I know things haven't been easy, but you've made huge strides with this Theo guy. So he didn't work out… but I don't want you to focus on that. Focus on the positive if you can."

"I'll try," Piper said, being agreeable but knowing deep down she didn't want another man, or to get back out into the dating pool.

After she disconnected the call, Piper did what she did best. She avoided her feelings, burying her head in the sand. If she had a spirit animal, it would be an ostrich. And she threw herself into completing the mock-ups, adding some extra touches, and using work to escape.

It had dawned on her while speaking with Caroline that Piper couldn't stay on the island. If she did, she would drown in memories of her time with Theo. As much as she wanted to remember him and their time together, right now she was too raw, too angry, too devastated. So she made plans, called the airline, and booked a flight home. She rescheduled her meeting with Jared for first thing in the morning. It would leave her with enough time to catch the afternoon flight to the west coast.

Piper stayed in her villa, at the kitchen table with her cameras and computer, working the day away. Any time she caught herself being overly emotional, she would squelch it. As long as she didn't feel, or think about him, she was fine. The one concession she made was to keep her phone with her. She told herself it was in case she needed to dial Caroline but that was a lie. She was waiting for Theo to call her back, to tell her she was being ridiculous, and that he wanted to apologize.

But he never called her back.

Chapter 13

"Piper, you outdid yourself with these, lass," Jared said, studying the brochure laid out on the conference table.

Looking down at the colorful menagerie in the attractive package she'd arranged, she could admit it was some damn fine work on her part. She said, "Thanks. Before you okay them, let these sit for twenty-four hours. Then I want you to look over them again and see if anything stands out that you want to modify. You can email me any changes that you might have, both for pictures and wording. Once I have those, it will just be a matter of my making the adjustments you want and then I will get you a final proof."

"I doubt I will have much, if anything, that I want to re-organize, but I understand your line of thought," Jared said, taking a seat and inviting her to do the same.

"Perfect. And after I develop the photos in my dark room at home, and have a full listing of artwork from the island, I will send you a detailed inventory for your records. I think, from what I've been able to shoot, I may have a full gallery showing," she explained. There would be at least one exhibition, if not more. And she was ready to purge the images from her cameras. Once she did that, she could look at her time there more objectively than emotionally.

"That's great, lass. I cannot wait to see what else you come up with if this is anything to judge by. You've done marvelous work and I look forward to seeing a gallery full of the images."

"You and Naomi will definitely need to come as my guests," Piper said, checking the time on her watch.

"That would be lovely. And I'm sure Naomi would get a kick out of it." Jared leaned back in his chair, his face shifting from jovial businessman to an expression of familial concern.

"Now, I hate to ask and even broach the topic, lass, but I need a run through of what occurred at the club the other night."

And here it was; part of what she had been dreading. Piper didn't want to remember the horrid scene she'd made, because that led to the break up with Theo. Then she would dissolve into tears or fury, and she just didn't want to feel anything right now.

"Jared, I'd rather not. I'm sorry that I caused such a stink, especially since the club was celebrating your engagement. I didn't mean to ruin that for you and Naomi. Please forgive me."

"Lass, I'm not worried about our engagement celebration but you and your well-being. It's part of my job as not only the owner of this place, but as your friend. Besides, you are not leaving the island until I'm certain you're okay and that Theo didn't physically hurt you to cause such a reaction. If he did, he will be punished. It's imperative that I know the truth of the matter."

She closed her eyes. Of course Jared would intervene and make sure nothing untoward had occurred, because he was a damn good Dom, and an even better friend.

"If you're trying to cover for Theo, don't. I don't care whether he's a Master or not, I'll not have any sub abused, and he will be dealt with swiftly," Jared went on.

"Jared, Sir, please it wasn't like that at all. Master Theo was trying to help me. Unfortunately, there are issues in my past tha I don't know can ever be fully healed."

Jared asked, "Are these issues the reason why you've neve scened in the DFC clubs before now?"

Piper was taken aback. It really shouldn't come as a surpris that the owners monitored people so closely, but it did. She didn' think anyone knew she avoided engaging in scenes. Sticking wit honesty, she admitted, "They are."

"And you're certain Theo did not harm you in any way? Jared pressed, searching her face for signs that she was being les than honest with him.

"Yes, I am," she replied. Physically she was fine, at least—a for emotionally, well, a broken heart meant she was still alive an could feel something for another human being, right? Jus because Theo couldn't stomach her nightmare in the end didn' mean he was a bad person or deserved to be disciplined by th club.

Jared contemplated her, his green gaze boring holes in he like he was attempting to read her soul.

"Thank you for telling me. Give yourself time and permis sion to continue working at it. I know I don't know what it wa that happened to you, but know that even the strongest of u break. And if Theo was helping you out that much, I have house in London you could stay in for a bit to continue the rela tionship, if you want."

Her heart ached and she fought back a fresh bout of tears She said, "I appreciate the offer, Master J, but I don't think that a good idea. I need to catch the ferry if I'm to make my fligh home. Thank you for your hospitality. I will be in touch."

She stood up from her seat and collected her bag, needing t escape. Jared gave her a big bear hug. "You as well, lass. Don't b a stranger, you are always welcome on the island."

"I appreciate it." She returned his embrace, blinking back th onslaught of tears. It would be some time before she could return to the island. Every place she looked, she saw Theo.

And she wanted to forget.

Piper left Jared's office, headed to the docks where her luggage had already been delivered, and boarded *The Surrender* with Master Shep at the helm. The boat got underway soon after she arrived. Piper didn't look back as the ferry sped away from the docks. There was no point. What was done, was done.

It didn't matter that she had found and lost her heart, all in the space of one week. Nor that the ever-present loneliness that dogged her everywhere she ventured was more pronounced now than it had ever been, and stretched out further than the unending blue waters of the Atlantic.

Chapter 14

He wiped a hand over his face, hoping to erase the stress of the last few days, and encountered almost two-and-a half weeks of beard growth. The last time he'd shaved was on his first day on Pleasure Island.

Bugger it.

Anytime he thought of Pleasure Island, Theo's mind veered toward Piper, and his heart squeezed. Time and an ocean lay between them. And Theo, who normally conquered and pursued what he wanted with vigor, stopped himself when it came to Piper. What if he had pushed her so far that she would no longer accept him as her Dom? In his hunger and need for dominance, he'd hurt her, and forgotten that he needed to protect her first and foremost, even from himself and his desires if need be. Theo, for all his knowledge and wisdom, his years spent becoming a Master, had never anticipated a woman like Piper.

There was no way to plan for someone like her, she had upended his paradigm and shaken the foundation of his stodgy, bleak existence.

Jacob shifted and Theo glanced at his son, his heart breaking over the pain he knew Jacob was in.

Since his return to London, Theo had spent his time at the hospital at Jacob's bedside and private room, staring at the gangly teenager, his leg wrapped in a cast and propped up, his mouth slightly open from his painkiller-induced sleep. His boy had undergone two surgeries on his left leg in the last ten days, and he'd handled them like a champ. As a parent, the worst thing was to see your child suffering and not be able to take it from them. And this wasn't a skinned knee Theo could bandage and make right with an ice cream cone.

Jacob's doctor was confident his injuries would fully heal. Although, he'd have to avoid the rugby field for a time. Theo and his mum would keep Jacob away from it, even if he had to lock the kid up in his dungeon to manage that. Theo had never before had such a stressful flight across the Atlantic, wondering if his son had made it out of surgery, not knowing the extent of his injuries. If Jacob's full recovery meant barring him from playing rugby, Theo would do so. Hell, Diane might even give him her blessing to lock him up in his private dungeon after this mishap.

The kid had a broken femur and torn ACL in his left leg. Both injuries would heal and, eventually, if he attended physiotherapy and completed rehabilitation, Jacob could return to the field. Two nurse technicians strolled in. Jacob gave them a sleepy nod when they explained that the doctor wanted some more X-rays and another series of tests to see how he was healing.

"We'll be back with him soon, sir."

"Thank you. I'll be here waiting for you, Jacob," Theo said.

Left to his own devices, Theo sipped on some tea and decided he'd been offline for far too long. Jacob was fine and finally out of the woods enough that Theo could focus on work a bit. Not that he was leaving his son's bedside anytime soon— Theo knew the solicitor team had him covered while he was taking care of Jacob.

In fact, Declan had given him a fully paid leave of absence through the end of the month. That way, in his words, "Apex will soldier on without you for the next few weeks. Focus on Jacob, Theo, the job's not what is important. And let me know if you need anything."

He could leave it, worry about his workload when he returned, but it was Theo who wanted to sift through the pile he had amassed after ten days in the hospital. Theo didn't plan to head back into the office until Jacob was on the road to recovery and being more of a nuisance than cause for concern, but that didn't mean he couldn't work from home. Besides, it was a nice distraction from worrying about Jacob, and then subsequently worrying about Piper.

Theo responded to emails until the nurses wheeled his sleeping child back into the room. Diane had left the hospital, heading home to take a shower, and meet the delivery van with the medical supplies they would need to bring him home. At least Theo's ex-wife had never kept Jacob from him. That was something for which he was eternally grateful.

With the panic and stress of the last few days lessening, Theo wondered about Piper. He knew he needed to contact her and explain where he'd been. Had she thought about him? Wondered about him? Missed him?

Christ, every time he thought of her, his heart ached. She visited him in his dreams during fitful bouts of sleep in the chair or the too-small couch in Jacob's room. When he woke, he reached for her, yearning to feel her in his arms. Who would have thought that, at his age, he would feel like an unschooled youth in love for the first time? And he did love her. She was willful, confident, expressive, and fierce, and every time she sank her claws in, it left him begging, hungering for more.

Would she want his love?

From his briefcase, Theo withdrew his office cell phone and switched the device on for the first time since arriving in London. He had a dozen or so messages, mainly from colleagues offering their aid in his family's time of crisis. However, there were two numbers that he didn't recognize and which weren't programmed into his phone. Theo listened through all his voice-mails, and his heart stopped when he reached those two messages. *Piper.* She'd called him, tried to get hold of him a week ago, but nothing since. She must think he was the worst sort of prick.

Sodding, buggery, shit!

"Bloody hell, Piper," he snarled to himself, feeling like a caged lion, unable to do anything about the colossal muck-up of their relationship.

"Girl troubles, Dad?" Jacob murmured, his voice groggy and laden with painkillers.

Theo shot Jacob a glance, marveling over how much he'd grown in the last year, looking more like himself every day. He asked, "Why would you say that?"

Jacob, rather high on his pain meds, gave him a cheeky grin and said, "Because you're normally so stoic and steady, so either it's a girl or it's a girl. Really, I'm only fifteen and know women are at the root of most of our troubles. Isn't that something you should already know, being the crusty old git that you are?"

Theo barked a laugh. Jacob had always been a pistol but with his inhibitions removed, he was hilarious. "And tell me, oh wise one, where this rather sound logic comes from?"

Jacob shrugged and gestured to his broken leg. "Because I wouldn't be lying here all banged up if I hadn't been show-boating during the match."

"So that was the way of it then, huh? What's her name?" Where had the time gone? Not long ago, Jacob would have been asking him to build forts and play ball, and now he was chasing girls. He had some way to go yet, but Theo could already see the man he would be. Jacob, his funny, sweet, determined, head-strong boy, on the cusp of manhood, and he couldn't be any prouder.

"Kate Winslow, with the most impressive rack and an arse

that won't quit." Jacob grinned and wiggled his eyebrows as he made an impression of said rack with his hands.

Bleeding hell; like father, like son. Theo wondered how much of his tastes Jacob would inherit.

"And you and this Kate, you're seeing each other?" he asked. By the time he was fifteen, he'd already shagged his steady girl friend. Maybe he and Jacob did need to sit down and discuss the finer points of sex education, more so than just ensuring he used protection.

"Not yet, but it will happen. Enough about Kate, what about this Piper woman, Dad? Why were you cursing her?"

Theo wasn't ready to discuss Piper with anyone, let alone his son. Especially not when he had bungled their relationship so horribly that she may never forgive him. If the shoe were on the other foot, he wasn't certain that he would forgive her. He said, "Jake, really it's—"

"None of my business? When are you going to realize you are my business? Dad, in all the years since you and Mum split, you've never dated anyone—not to my recollection. At least never anyone that you mentioned around me. So it stands to reason if you are sitting there cursing her, she must be pretty important."

Jacob had hit the nail on the head, staring at him with an eyebrow raised, waiting for Theo's response. He asked his son, "When did you get so wise?"

Jacob shrugged. "It happens. So, when do I get to meet her?"

"It wouldn't bother you, my bringing a woman home? I know we've never discussed this, but I've always tried to shield you, and wanted you to have as normal a childhood as possible with your mum and me not being together." Maybe Theo had gone to extremes, but he'd never wanted to lose Jacob. His son was the most important part of his world, and perhaps he'd wanted to make it up to him for being the one to split their family apart. Guilt has a funny way of making us do things. Theo had used the stipulation Diane had placed upon him regarding keeping his lifestyle choices hidden as a crutch not to get emotionally attached.

"Of course it wouldn't. Although, if you must know, I don't want an evil stepmother type, and would tell you right off if she was dodgy in any way, but I want you happy, Dad. What are you going to do with yourself when I go away to university? Continue to grow callouses?"

Jacob was making masturbation jokes now? It made Theo feel old. He was just glad Diane wasn't in the room. As for Piper, he said to Jacob, "I'm not sure she wants to hear from me. We kind of left it off in a bad spot. Besides, she lives in the US, so it's not an easy fix."

"Then stop being a tosser and call her. And where does she live in America? If you and she were to live together, there are a few American colleges I'm interested in attending that I might be able to get into more easily if you were already there."

"Wait, you want to go to university in America? Does your mum know? I'm not sure I like the thought of you being that far away from home." And how in the sodding hell was his son old enough and wise enough to give him sound dating advice?

"That's another talk for another time. I'm quite tired. Call Piper, Dad, and apologize for being a tosser." Jacob's eyes drooped as he deflected Theo's inquiry.

Theo wasn't certain whether he should feel proud or horrified that at fifteen, Jacob understood the diversion tactic it took seasoned solicitors years to master. As for Piper, he wasn't convinced.

"You think she'll forgive me, huh?" Theo asked, uncertainty lacing his voice and his heart.

"Like you have always told me whenever I was hesitant to try something I feared, you will never know unless you try." Jacob yawned and his eyes slid closed.

Love swamped Theo for this boy—this young man—he had

somehow been lucky enough to have as his son. "I love you, Jake. Always and forever."

"You too, Dad." And then Jacob's face went slack-jawed as the painkiller infiltrated his system and he was out cold with the drug.

Jacob was right. Theo wouldn't know unless he contacted Piper, laid his cards out on the table, and apologized profusely for being such a daft prick. Piper was his submissive, damnit, and he planned to claim her once and for all.

Theo considered his options, and the different maneuvers he might need to implement with Piper as he watched over Jacob until Diane returned. How much did he want from Piper? He loved her. Could he forgo clubs to be with her? Absolutely, there was no question about that. It wasn't like he had placed much importance upon attending them frequently anyway. And it wasn't as if the offerings had enticed him enough to want to play with a submissive more than once. He didn't want another submissive in his bed, he wanted Piper. The thought of anyone else in his bed stopped him cold.

If she told him to get lost, he would keep going back until she forgave him. Theo wouldn't take no for an answer. She was the submissive for him, and he was her Dom. He just had to convince her of that.

"How is he?" Diane asked when she returned. She was still a lovely woman, petite, trim, with fine lines near her eyes, which resembled Jacob's in form and color.

"Good. They did some more X-rays, but he slept for most of the time you were away. Did you get all the medical equipment settled?"

"Yes, Don's at home getting his room arranged now," she murmured, never taking her eyes off their son.

"You're a great mum, Diane, always have been."

She blushed becomingly and gave him a look. "Thank you, Theo. I know how much you've given up for him. He does, too.

And I know I didn't make it easy on you in the beginning and am sorry for that, but you've always been there for Jacob. I appreciate everything you've always done for him. Why don't you go get yourself a shower and some sleep? I can take over for a bit."

"Perhaps. I have a call to make but will be back straight away."

"Take your time," she said, sitting in the chair at Jacob's bedside.

Theo strolled out of Jacob's room and headed outside. He didn't want anyone to overhear his conversation. He tried calling both of Piper's numbers, but each rolled over to voicemail. *Damnit, Piper.* She probably saw it was him and was avoiding answering. That meant he'd have to do something drastic to get her attention.

Theo checked the time and tried Jared's number.

"Theo, to what do I owe the pleasure? How's Jacob?" Jared asked.

Theo said, "He's good. On the mend and will be back on the rugby field in no time. Is Piper still on the island?" He had to figure out where his quarry was first. Then he could put his plan into motion.

"No. She left the island shortly after you did. What the hell happened with her, man? She wouldn't tell me the details on the bad club scene other than to defend you. If I hadn't corroborated her story with the nearby club attendees that night, I would have said she had Stockholm syndrome."

"Bloody hell. I already told you that—we tried pushing her boundaries on an issue of hers and it failed. It's water under the bridge. Where can I find her? And no, it's none of your god damn business why I need to contact my sub."

"Your sub, huh? Piper resides in Santa Barbara and has her gallery there. I'll email you her business address, but not her home one. That, she will have to invite you to herself, and I will leave it up to her whether she chooses to do so or not."

"Thanks for not making it easy, you wanker. How did she seem when she left Pleasure Island?"

"Like someone had kicked her puppy, if you must know."

Shit. He had been afraid of that.

"Thanks, J, I owe you one," he said as he hung up. Then he cursed himself for his bungling.

He went back inside the hospital and up to Jacob's room. He would give it another two days, assist Diane with Jacob's transfer home, and be sure Jake had no relapses before he made his move with Piper. That way he could ensure his ex-wife could handle Jacob's care on her own for a few days.

Chapter 15

Damn, *blasted Brit.*

Two weeks later, and she couldn't seem to go an hour with him entering her mind. Piper didn't want him there—or anywhere else, for that matter. She wanted him out of her mind, her dreams, and most importantly, her heart. No good would come from pining for a man who didn't feel the same way. For Theo, it might have been a simple arrangement and scratching an itch. For Piper, Theo had managed to wiggle his way inside her heart, and it was crushing to realize that she had been so easy to set aside.

Images from the secluded beach on Pleasure Island came into focus on the proof sheet. The brilliance and profusion of color was like an antithesis to the solemn acceptance of her fate, as a woman destined to live her life alone. She'd been right in her estimation. Pleasure Island had been a font of photographs, each one more breathtaking than the next. There was a distinct possibility she might have to have more than one gallery showing. She also was toying with the idea of creating a book of her photos to sell in her gallery and bookstores.

Maybe it was too lofty a dream, but it was an idea she held

on to with every print from Pleasure Island that she developed. It made it easier to focus on that instead of the pressure building in her chest. One more roll to develop into contact prints, then she would head into the gallery. Her assistant, Megan, was an absolute wonder, and would take care of anything that came up until she arrived, so Piper wasn't worried there. There were a few of the prints that she wanted to play with and enlarge, add some toning to them. These were just contact prints, anyhow. The real magic began after she'd developed those. It gave her a base starting point where she could determine which prints to enlarge and which not to.

In the two weeks she'd been home, Piper had spent nearly every waking moment doing what she did best; work. It was the only way she could survive, especially those first few days between her tears and two more episodes that reared their ugly heads. Real nasty ones, too, which Caroline had explained were likely due to the stress of her heartache. Her therapist's recommendation was that Piper relax and take it easy for a little while but then plunge back into the BDSM scene to find another Dom. But Piper didn't want another Dom, not after the last one. Her heart was far too raw. Instead of following Caroline's suggestions, Piper split her time between the darkroom here at her home in the Santa Barbara hills, and the one in her gallery, Phoenix Rising Photography, located on State Street in the Paseo Nuevo Mall.

Piper placed the film negatives and print paper in the contact printer to create her proof sheets. From there, she'd be able to determine the sizes, textures, and exposure value. She knew the steps to take as if they were burned into her cerebral cortex. She preferred this old school method for the purity of the prints, the fidelity to the original image, and the exquisite detail.

As the proof sheet developed, a lightning bolt of agony lanced through her chest. Theo's handsome face appeared candid, up close, his eyes heavy-lidded with passion and a sensual half-smirk shrouding his lips as he stared up at her while they were in bed. He was such a beautiful man. Instead of heading into the gallery, a sense of urgency descended upon her and she realized she had to develop the rest. With her heart urging her onward, Piper created eight by ten portraits from the negatives. One after another, they were all of Theo, with his carnal, I'm-gonna-make-you-scream-as-you-climax-and-beg-for-more expression. Piper's body throbbed in remembrance and a sudden onslaught of unrequited sexual frustration.

Damn him.

Even a simple photograph of the Brit could make her hotter than a heat wave along the San Andreas fault line.

She developed print after print of the two of them kissing, of Theo's face just as he entered her, and one of her, her head tossed back in ecstasy, the lines of her body taut as his cock plunged deep—one he had snapped. By the time she had finished creating the entire roll she'd taken that morning, Piper was shaking as though a magnitude eight quake was rumbling the ground beneath her. Theo. She didn't want to love him, but she did—more than she had thought herself capable of loving another. Walls she'd begun erecting crumbled as the seismic wave continued its swath of devastation through her system. The photographs slashed at her composure and, in a blink, her heart shattered into a billion pieces once again.

This wasn't something she was just going to get over. He wasn't someone she was going to get over, just wake up one day and realize she no longer loved him. That wasn't how it worked —not for Piper, at least. She took her time, inhaling some deep yoga breaths before rising from the spot on the floor where she'd curled into a ball.

Still clutching one of his images in her hand, she glanced at her watch and flinched. Shit, she was horrendously tardy. Piper collected each image of Theo and placed them all into a manila file folder. After making sure the place was tidy, with her chemicals and supplies stowed in the proper places, Piper exited the darkroom clutching Theo's file. She laid it on the center island in her kitchen. As much as a part of her knew she should toss the pictures, negatives and all, she couldn't bring herself to throw them away. Maybe after some time they would bring her comfort and joy instead of devastating sorrow.

Not to mention, they were the only thing she had to remember him by, and as much as she wanted to forget because of the despair filling her heart, if she tossed them away, it would be as if their time together had never existed. And she didn't know what would be worse: the pain, or having no memory of it.

Instead of making a decision, she left the file on the counter and headed to the gallery. From her house up in the hills, it took her about twenty minutes to get there, depending upon traffic. She adored downtown Santa Barbara with its Spanish influences, red tile roofs, and palm trees, with the harbor and beach nearby. Her gallery was located in one of the heavy touristy malls on State Street and garnered a ton of foot traffic. As it was a Tuesday, during the school year, traffic was lighter. Summer was her busy season, on top of the Christmas holidays and any exhibitions.

As soon as Piper made it into the gallery, she sent her assistant to lunch and went through her mail at the front desk.

"Thanks so much. I was so hungry, I was ready to start eating my arm off. And I got you something," Megan, her twenty-five-year-old assistant said, beaming as she returned from her lunch break. Piper liked the spunky, petite redhead who was always dressed in the latest fashion trends. She kind of felt a bit like Megan's big sister at times instead of her boss, but the girl knew her stuff, was punctual, organized, and a deep in the bones good person. Piper didn't know what she had ever done without her.

"You did? That's so sweet of you, Megan, you didn't have to do that."

"I know, but I thought you could use a little pick me up.

You've been so down lately," Megan said, handing her a small pastry bag.

"Is this what I think it is?" Piper asked, gladly accepting the small bag as the scent of chocolate reached her nose.

Megan gave her a sly grin. "Yep. You can thank me later."

"Oh sweet heavens, chocolate eclairs and café au lait from *Le Macaron*. Have I told you how you're the best assistant in the world?"

"More than once. But it's nice to see a smile on your face again for a change."

"I have had my panties in a twist here lately, haven't I? Sorry about that. I promise to get myself out of my funk, starting with these beauties. Now that you're back, I have some work in the back to see to."

"Go," Megan shooed her away with her hands, "I've got this, we aren't busy. And if I need you, I'll come get you."

"Thanks, Megan." Piper exited the sales floor and headed to her office. Her heartbreak was beginning to develop into another handicap. Did she want another reason to keep people away? Maybe the problem wasn't them, but her own outlook. She'd been starting to feel restless, with a need to experience a new place she could travel to. Work clearly hadn't been the answer, nor had it kept the heartbreak at bay if her assistant was feeling so sorry for her that she had bought her chocolate. Maybe what she really needed was some time off. Her therapist was constantly harassing her to take a vacation. Perhaps she had a point.

Instead of tackling the stack of bills that had piled up over the last few weeks, Piper pulled out her huge accordion style file folder that contained brochures for places she still hadn't visited. They were all alphabetized, of course, and when she flipped the top open, Alaska stood out first.

Hmmm, it wasn't too late in the year to do a small ship cruise into the interior. It would be cold, no doubt, but the scenery would be extraordinary.

Piper spent the next hour or so munching on the eclairs, searching through brochures, and scouring the internet for decent flights. Excitement threaded through her veins. She'd get some new photos in, perhaps she could even have a showing just on the Alaska trip. Even though this would be a vacation, she'd still have her camera with her. She never left home without it.

This was what she needed, an infusion of new adventures and new horizons to shake her from her maudlin, mopey existence. Heartbreak, who needed it? Not this girl, that was for damn sure. She was smiling at her computer screen when Megan knocked on her office door and poked her head in.

"What's up?" Piper asked.

"There's a customer interested in purchasing *Horizon Glory*, but they would like to speak with the artist first," Megan explained.

It happened more often than not, especially when Piper was here. *Horizon Glory*, that was one of the new prints from Pleasure Island. They'd added the piece this week. Well, good, the sooner she sold the island prints, the better. And Jared would certainly be pleased, especially if this was a foreshadowing of how well a full gallery showing of the island pictures would do. She said, "Tell them I will be right out."

"Perfect. Will do, boss," Megan replied, heading back to the sales floor.

Piper pulled out her compact mirror from her top desk drawer. She made sure she didn't have any chocolate smudges on her face anywhere and then added a touch of lip gloss. It was her standard operating procedure. After a mortifying experience with one of silicon valley's tech giants and an unfortunate piece of spinach between her teeth, she always double-checked her appearance before meeting a potential buyer.

Piper entered the showroom floor just as Megan said, "You're all set, Mr. Brown. Here's your bill of sale, and the shipping

nformation. I will email you once your artwork is en route with
ill the tracking and customs information."

"Thank you, Megan. You've been a delight," said a deep,
cultured male voice.

Piper stopped dead in her tracks. It was the voice she heard
nightly in her dreams. The hint of a British accent, the deep
paritone, how it made her think of brandy and cigars. His back
was to her, his broad shoulders accentuated by a crisp, white
dress shirt. She would know his silhouette anywhere.

Why was he here? What did he want? She stood frozen to the
spot, like her feet had been cemented to the wooden floor. But
inside, her panic button had sounded the alarm. Did she have
ime to escape? She didn't want to see him. She didn't want him
to know how much he'd hurt her. And she had the very real fear
that she would cave, that she wasn't strong enough to turn away
from him. Piper couldn't be some casual screw to whom he came
knocking on her door anytime he got a hankering.

Piper was about to dash back into the storeroom.

"And here's the artist, Piper Delaney," Megan said, beaming
over the sale, and gesturing toward her. Piper prayed for a sink-
hole to open up as Theo swiveled around and the full impact of
his energy hit her.

His enigmatic cinnamon gaze was a one-two punch to her
solar plexus, and it was as though all the air was sucked from the
room. If it were possible, he was even more handsome and
dashing in his slacks and dress shirt, looking every inch the businessman. Her eyes soaked up every nuance. His hair was a mite
longer. His beard neatly trimmed, with some new specs of gray
dotting the dark hair.

Her heart thumped madly in her breast. What should she do
now that he had seen her? She couldn't run back into the storeroom without causing a scene. Indecision plagued her, rendering
her immobile. She couldn't even pretend to smile at him. Tears

threatened to fall, and she diverted the majority of her energy into keeping those under wraps.

When she didn't move, when she couldn't, it was Theo who broke through the stillness and approached. His long-legged stride ate up the distance between them, and every part of her system was attuned to his every nuance. He crowded her space, leaving a mere foot between them.

"Miss Delaney, it's a pleasure. Theo Brown at your service." His voice softened at the use of the term 'pleasure' and her heart trembled. Then he held up his hand for her to shake. She stared at him, at his hand, like he was an alien come down to plane Earth, holding out a strange tentacle.

"Piper, love, shake my hand lest you cause a scene before your employee," Theo murmured, with the barest hint of a command. At his blatant use of the endearment, rage and heart break surfaced in suffocating tidal waves. The fact that he could show up here after all this time and pretend like nothing was amiss!

Screw that—and him, for that matter.

Instead of accepting his hand, she backed away from him. It was more like she stormed back through the doorway to her office, with Megan looking at her like she'd grown an extra head but Piper couldn't worry about that right now. She was going to lock herself in her office if need be, until he was gone. She'd leave the gallery if she had to.

Except Theo was hot on her tail, barely a step behind her. His fingers wrapped around her arm, stalling her forward progression as he yanked her into his arms. Before she could escape out the back door, he had her back pressed up against it. Then he was kissing her, commanding a response from her, devastating her with his lips and his touch as he pressed his length against her.

Her body rejoiced at his touch. The man kissed her with his entire being, plundering her mouth, stealing her reason and logic until her entire world boiled down to Theo. She couldn't have stopped herself from kissing him back if she'd tried. As desire bombarded her system, it unleashed a rage so potent and fierce, she bit down on his bottom lip.

"Yeow, fuck, Piper!" Theo barked, his gaze accusing and all stern Dom. She didn't care. He could brood all he wanted to, *she* got to say when he touched her.

"You don't get to walk in here all willy-nilly after not a word from you in two weeks and touch me. Got it?" She shoved against his chest for emphasis.

"Careful, love, we need to talk," Theo said, his gaze obviously attempting to pierce the invisible shields she'd erected.

Maybe they did need to have it out, whatever the outcome might be. Perhaps that was the key for Piper to finally get over him and move on. They'd already put on a show for Megan, who no doubt would ply her with a million questions the first chance she had.

"Not here," Piper said as she delved into her courage and tried to assuage the raging fury and heartbreak swimming in her chest. She would do it. Hear whatever he felt was necessary to fly a few thousand miles to say, and remain unaffected, then she would send him on his way. "You can follow me to my house."

"I'll be right behind you," he said, the promise in his eyes.

She just bet he would. There was no point in trying to lose his BMW on the winding roads up to her home. It was better this way, that they air everything out. Then she could move on with her life.

Then she could begin the process of falling out of love with him.

Chapter 16

She looked even better than he remembered.

Theo followed Piper's silver Mercedes up a winding cliffside road to her home, a buttercream colored, ranch style house. He parked his rental car in the driveway behind her vehicle, then followed her in. Her home was a reflection of her. It had a wooden vaulted ceiling with exposed golden pinewood beams a shade darker than the hardwood floors throughout the place. Along one entire side of the house were floor to ceiling windows, overlooking her pool and the hills and valleys overlooking the city of Santa Barbara. It was a beautiful place and it suited Piper. The open, airy space overlooking the mountains. The secluded nature of it. It was very much like the woman herself—an extension of her.

"Your home is lovely, Piper," Theo said, following her into the kitchen with its shiny silver stainless steel appliances and forest green marble countertops. Now that he had her all to himself, he wasn't letting her get away. He had been stupid and ignorant on the island, more concerned with his own sense of self-righteous indignation than his sub's pain.

"Thank you. Why are you here, Theo?" she said, leaning

back against the counter and putting the kitchen island between them. He didn't miss the symbolism of it, or the way she held herself away from him.

No matter the outcome, he owed her this much, needed to explain. He said, "I came to apologize. I should have told you I was leaving the island, and more importantly, why. I'm sorry it's taken me so long to reach you."

She held up a hand, guilt contorting her beautiful face. "I know I handled things poorly that night you wanted to do a scene with me. I'm sorry. I didn't mean to get so worked up afterward, and I didn't mean to make you leave the island to prove your point. I just—"

His heart squeezed at the damage he'd done. "Piper, I didn't leave the island because we had one scene not go well. I'm made of sterner stuff than that. At least, I'd like to think so, and I had every intention of apologizing for pushing you before you were ready. We were still building trust between us. In my enthusiasm to your responses—but also because I wanted you to be mine completely, and thought such a scene would solidify the bond between us—I pushed before you were ready. So, when the time came, I didn't think of you that night, but me, and what I thought you needed, so I overlooked the signs that your body was clearly sending me. For that, I am so unimaginably sorry, and still hope that you will give me the chance to atone for my sins that night. But no, you weren't the reason I left the island so suddenly, love. My son, Jacob, was injured in an accident. His mum called me from the hospital as they were taking him in to surgery."

Concern dotted her face and she said, "Oh god. Is he okay? I didn't know, no one told me. I'm so sorry, I just assumed…"

"Yes, he's recovering at home, finally. It was an unfortunate rugby accident; broken leg, torn ACL and some bruises, but after two surgeries, he's healing. I didn't get your messages right away, and I'm sorry for that. I didn't have my work cell phone with me, only my personal one. I'll have to make sure you have the number for it in the future."

She shook her head and said, "I don't think that will be necessary. I'm glad Jacob is okay but you didn't need to come all this way to tell me this. A phone call would have sufficed."

Theo had prepared himself on the long flight that she might not want him, that he had once again miscalculated. However, he wasn't ready to throw in the towel just yet, and knew he'd have to lay all of his cards on the table. Drawing on his courage, he glanced down. On top of the green marble, Theo spied a file. He flipped it open.

"Wait, don't," she protested, trying to keep him from looking inside. But it was too late. Theo almost laughed at what he discovered. Joy hummed and spread inside his chest. He'd been worried that she didn't want him or wouldn't accept him, but as he stared at his own face, at the images she'd printed and kept, seeing one of the two of them kissing, relief flooded his veins and hope surged in his chest. Piper was his submissive, and even if it meant he had to split his time between her place and his, they would make it work. He would make it work because he could no longer see his life without her in it.

"Why did you keep these?" He nodded toward the photos.

"You weren't supposed to see those." She bowed her head, but not before he spied tears glistening in her eyes.

His heart hammered in his chest as he moved around the island and caged her against the countertop with his arms. He murmured, "If we are going to make this work between us, we need honesty from each other. It's one of the reasons why my marriage to Jacob's mother didn't work out. I won't go back to living a lie. I want you, Piper. I want you so much, I ache when you're not with me. Tell me why you kept the photos."

FEAR DANCED with hope in her chest. It came down to her deciding what she wanted in her life, for her life. His scent intoxicated her and she wanted to curl into his nearness, into his body, and feel his arms around her again. When push came to shove, there really was no choice at all.

She loved him.

What more was there to debate? He hadn't abandoned her but had left to take care of his injured son. Any anger she'd had evaporated as if it had never existed. Theo was the only man, the only Dom, she wanted to give her whole heart to and gift with her submission. Peace settled over Piper's being as she made her decision. No matter the outcome, the anxiety that had been building in her chest relaxed and subsided.

"Piper, talk to me, love. Did I ruin everything between us at the club that night?"

She shook her head and finally answered him. "No. You didn't. It would have been easier if you had, but I was as much to blame for that night. If I had been honest with you about what happened to me, then maybe we could have avoided it. I kept your images so I would have something to remember you by. I thought you decided I was too much, that my past was too much for you, and you opted out of the relationship with your departure."

He tilted her face up until their gazes clashed. "Do you really think so little of me that you would believe I would toss you aside like that without saying a word?" he said.

"It's happened to me before and it's all I really know, Theo. I wanted to believe that you were different but when I didn't hear from you, I just assumed you didn't want me anymore."

Both of his hands cradled her face and in his eyes, she saw such naked emotion, her heart trembled. "Piper, you're incredible to have survived what you did, to be as warm and inviting as you are. There's no place I'd rather be than in your arms. And as for clubs, those don't matter. I haven't been big into the club scene in years. It doesn't mean I don't want to help you past tha fear, but I'm willing to work with you on it and take the tim needed. And if we don't ever get there, we don't. Those thing don't matter to me. You do. As long as you'll still have me, accep me as your Dom."

With her heart trembling and hope swirling in her chest, sh said, "You want to be with me?"

"Piper, my life was rather staid and boring before you cam along. I wasn't unhappy but I was comfortable being just a fathe and a workaholic. It was far easier than putting myself back ou there. But then you barreled into my life and made me see jus how lonely and closed off I'd become. You brought sunshine int my life when all that had been present were gray skies and rain Do I want to be with you? That's like asking if I want air t breathe. I can't imagine my life without you in it. I love you."

"You really do?" she said, amazement and disbelief cloudin her voice. Theo loved her, even knowing about her past and he deficiencies. He was willing to put aside attending clubs an public scenes to be with her. Tears rained down her face as sh stared into his eyes. She didn't know what she'd done to deserv him.

He stroked her cheeks with his thumbs, catching her tear "Yeah, I do. What do you say, love, are you going to take chance on a boring sod like me?"

"Theo, I…" The words seemed to lodge themselves in he throat so she planted her lips over his, pouring her heart and he soul into his capable, loving hands. He effusively returned he kiss, growling into her mouth, and taking it deeper until he every breath came from him. Piper wrapped her arms aroun him, plastering her body to his until there was no space betwee them.

It was Theo who released her at length, his thumb strokin, over her lower lip. "Was that a yes? I need you to spell it out fo me, love, so that there are no further misunderstandings."

"Yes. I love you. There's no other Dom for me."

His smile took her breath away. And then his lips did the same as they claimed hers for a soul-deep caress. Piper melted into his embrace, kissing him back with all the love she felt for him. His hungry lips swallowed her moans as the kiss heated, stoking flames of desire at the torrid mingling. It felt like months had passed since she'd felt him and she couldn't seem to get close enough to him, needing to be closer to him, feel his skin against hers. Theo hoisted her into his arms and she went willingly, wrapping her legs around his waist as he carried her to an unforeseen destination.

"Bedroom?" he asked, sucking her earlobe into his mouth.

"Back there." She flailed her arm behind her and then resumed their kiss. She trusted he would get them where they needed to be. But she never wanted to stop kissing him. They entered her bedroom and she helped him strip her blouse off. She tore at his dress shirt, eager to feel his flesh beneath her hands. Buttons flew off, pinging across the room. He chuckled darkly.

And then he groaned as her hand slid beneath his slacks and gripped his cock.

"Christ, love."

"Hurry. I need you, right now. We can worry about finesse later," she said, her breath shuddering out in short, shallow pants. She squeezed his shaft, stroking his firm flesh.

"Good call." He laid her on the bed, shucking his pants and boxers, while she shoved off her skirt and panties. Then she opened her arms and he was there, following her down, and kissing her like he needed her in order to breathe.

He settled his large form between her thighs. She grasped his shaft, fitting him at her entrance. With their gazes locked on each other, he thrust, and his cock furrowed inside her clasping channel until he was seated to the hilt. They held still, his shaft embedded inside her, connecting them as they stared into each other's eyes, feeling the love they each found in the other. Theo rolled his hips, stroking his length inside her heat. She moaned into his mouth as she kissed him, meeting his thrusts, surrendering to the passion, and yes, the love between them. She had ached when she'd thought she had lost him forever and now she overflowed with him, his love, his steadfast heart, and she gave him everything.

She undulated her pelvis, meeting his fervent thrusts again and again as they made love. Over and over, he rose above her, holding her close as he made her body soar to the heavens. She clasped him tightly, her nails digging in to his muscled back, sliding down to his tight rear, and holding on as he plowed through all of her defenses until her whole world boiled down to him.

He thrust and she met him each time as the tempo of their lovemaking accelerated. She moaned and arched her back as pleasure scored her system.

"Oh, Theo," she cried into his mouth as her climax blasted through her. She clung to him as her body tremored and shook, her pussy clenching at his cock. He strained in her arms.

"Piper," he groaned. His shaft jolted and a warmth flooded her channel as his cum poured inside her.

In the hazy afterglow of their lovemaking, Theo kept himself between her thighs, stroking her face. "I do love you, Piper. I don't want to live without you ever again. I want you warming my bed every day and every night."

"I don't think I will ever get tired of hearing you say those words. Especially when I'm so in love with you, but I'm worried that we live so far apart. You live in London, I live here."

He smiled, shrugging his shoulders. "So we make it work. We'll split time between our places and go from there. We'll make it work, love, because I want you more than I want air to breathe. Why don't you come to London with me for a bit? I'd like to introduce you to my son. And I know Jacob would like to meet you."

Knowing how much his son mattered to him, the fact that he wanted her to know him spoke volumes to Piper and waylaid any lingering doubts she might have had. Stroking her hands down his back, she said, "I'd like that. I will need to find a darkroom so I can work."

He kissed her nose. "I had a feeling you might say something like that. And I have a contractor standing by to make modifications to a room in my house for you."

"Really? You were so certain?"

"No, I wasn't. I just knew what I felt for you was true, and I believed that you felt the same way after your messages."

"I do love you, Theo, so much. I can't believe you would do that for me," she said, love for him swamping her. She never dreamed that she would feel this happy and complete, and all of it was because of this wonderful man.

"Because I want all of you, love, I want you happy and with me. It's just a room, and I figure we can spend time here, too."

"You really thought of everything?"

He gave her a sexy grin, his eyes intense as he said, "I did. I'm a solicitor, it's what we do. Oh, and you'll have to marry me so that you are legally bound to me. I won't take no for an answer."

"Are you proposing then?" She gasped as he rocked his hips, and she discovered his recuperative powers were more than up to the challenge as his shaft hardened and lengthened inside her once more.

"No, I'm giving you the rundown so you understand I'll not only be your Dom but your lawful Master from here on out. You will have to obey me." He wiggled his brows.

"In your dreams, Sir."

"My life is never going to be dull again."

She gripped him tight, pleasure radiating from her being as his shaft plunged to the hilt. "Not if I can help it."

"I couldn't ask for anything more." And then he claimed her lips in a torrid, hungry kiss.

After all the pain, and sorrow, and the years of loneliness, Piper surrendered everything to the one Dom who had made all the long, lonely years worthwhile. The road she'd had to travel to reach him—even the horrors involved—had all led her to this time, this place, and this man: her Dom, her everything. She wouldn't trade a thing, not when he was her reward. She wondered how he would feel about a Vegas wedding on their way to his home in London.

Now that he was hers, she was never letting him go.

Epilogue

Three years later...

Two hundred royal blue graduation caps were tossed into the air, sending the crowd into an effusive fit of cheers.

Piper glanced out over the soccer field as the wind blew, rocking Nora against her breast. She was being fussy, today of all days, when her big brother was graduating. They waited for Jacob, in his cap and gown, to find them near the back edge of the crowd.

She peeked at the now sleeping bundle in her arms. At five months, Nora and her twin sister, Nina, were giving her and Theo a run for their money. Their little miracle twins that modern medicine had helped them have. There were tears in her husband's eyes today. The only other time she'd seen him cry had been when he'd held their daughters for the first time.

As the crowd began to disperse, Jacob located them. His mom, Diane, and her husband, Don, followed closely behind him, beaming in their pride at his accomplishment. Theo hugged his son, patting him on the back in his joy.

"Congrats, Jake. I'm so proud of you," Theo said as Jacob,

now as tall as his dad, pulled back with a huge grin on his handsome face.

"Thanks, Dad. And how are my sisters this morning, Piper?" Jacob said. He looked more and more like the spitting image of his father every day. It had taken the two of them a bit in the beginning, but Piper had grown to love her stepson dearly. And he absolutely doted on his baby sisters.

"Being fussy," she said, standing up from her seat and giving him a one-armed hug while cradling Nora in the other. "I'm so happy for you, Jacob. Congratulations."

"Thank you, Piper."

"Picture time," Diane chimed in, nearly dancing in her excitement.

Piper placed her sleeping bundle in the buggy beside Nina. Fresh air always made Nina conk out and sleep like the dead. She'd be more worried if Theo wasn't there to tell her it was totally normal when babies had a lot of fresh air.

"I can do those for you," Piper said, pushing the dual stroller over.

"Oh, if you wouldn't mind," Diane said, handing over her camera.

"Not at all." Piper already had her Nikon set up. After all, she was the photographer in the bunch, promising profusely to send Diane all the images she'd snapped with her camera as well as Diane's. She took ones of Jacob with his mom, with his mom and step-dad, with his mom and dad, with just his dad.

Nina and Nora woke up just in time to have their picture taken with their big brother. Piper got the three of them, and then a few with their dad.

"Now we should get one of the whole family," Jacob said, directing the show a bit, what with his parents blubbering all over the place.

Piper adjusted her camera lens, setting the focus once everyone was in position to make sure she got everyone. Then

Jacob transferred Nina to her father's arms and repositioned Nora in his, and then said, "You too, Piper, we need the whole family for this one."

Tears welled up instantly in her eyes. Since the girls' arrival, she'd turned into a blubberer. She glanced at the group, with Theo holding Nina and a hand out toward her, his love shining in his eyes. Even Diane and Don were waving her over. She nodded and blinked back her tears, then set the timer on her camera and strode over to Theo's outstretched arm.

Piper, who had once believed she would live a lonely existence, slid into her husband's arm and smiled just as the camera clicked, capturing her family.

THE END

Anya Summers

Born in St. Louis, Missouri, Anya grew up listening to Cardinals baseball and reading anything she could get her hands on. She remembers her mother saying if only she would read the right type of books instead binging her way through the romance aisles at the bookstore, she'd have been a doctor. While Anya never did get that doctorate, she graduated cum laude from the University of Missouri-St. Louis with an M.A. in History.

Anya is a bestselling and award-winning author published in multiple fiction genres. She also writes urban fantasy and paranormal romance under the name Maggie Mae Gallagher. A total geek at her core, when she is not writing, she adores attending the latest comic con or spending time with her family. She currently lives in the Midwest with her two furry felines.

Don't miss these exciting titles by Anya Summers and Blushing Books!

The Dungeon Fantasy Club Collection
The complete set of all eight full-length, scintillating, spicy romance novels!
Her Highland Master
To Master and Defend
Two Doms for Kara
His Driven Domme
Her Country Master
Love Me, Master Me
Submit to Me

Her Wired Dom

The Pleasure Island Collection
The complete set of nine full-length novels!
Her Master and Commander, Book 1
Her Music Masters, Book 2
Their Shy Submissive, (Novella) Book 3
Her Lawful Master, Book 4
Her Rockstar Dom, Book 5
Duets and Dominance, Book 6
Her Undercover Doms (Novella) Book 7
Ménage in Paradise, Book 8
Her Rodeo Masters, Book 9

Cuffs and Spurs Series
His Scandalous Love, Book 1
His Unexpected Love, Book 2
His Wicked Love, Book 3
His Untamed Love, Book 4
His Tempting Love, Book 5
His Seductive Love, Book 6
His Secret Love, Book 7
His Cherished Love, Book 8

Crescent City Kings Series
Lone Survivor, Book 1

Alcyran Chronicles Series
Taken By The Beast, Book 1
Claimed By The Beast, Book 2
Loved By The Beast, Book 3

Audio Books
Her Highland Master

Visit her on social media here:
http://www.facebook.com/AnyaSummersAuthor
Twitter: @AnyaBSummers
Goodreads: https://www.goodreads.com/author/show/
15183606.Anya_Summers
Sign-up for Anya Summers Newsletter

Connect with Anya Summers:
www.anyasummers.com

Blushing Books

Blushing Books is one of the oldest eBook publishers on the web. We've been running websites that publish spanking and BDSM related romance and erotica since 1999, and we have been selling eBooks since 2003. We hope you'll check out our hundreds of offerings at http://www.blushingbooks.com.

Blushing Books Newsletter

Please subscribe to the Blushing Books newsletter to receive updates & special promotional offers.

You can also join by using your mobile phone: Just text BLUSHING to 22828.